London, in Limbo

Shaun Girling

Published by Shaun Girling, 2013.

This is a work of fiction. Similarities to real people, places, or events are entirely coincidental.

LONDON, IN LIMBO

First edition. March 25, 2013.

ISBN: 979-8223090120

Written by Shaun Girling.

London, in Limbo
by Shaun Girling
Copyright 2013 Shaun Girling
Smashwords Edition

Chapter 1

I was on the phone to her the first time I visited The Kennedys. Actually, it was more like a duck under a shower than a visit. I didn't relish spilling out my feelings at the bus stop for old ladies and Australian tourists to hear and I sought refuge in the back streets. It was evening, pouring down and the café looked inviting with soft light embracing the pavement. As I approached, I glimpsed through the window a family of figures gathered around one table as if it were an open fire. Whatever they were doing held their attention and distracted me from the hell that was engulfing my life.

As I caught my reflection in the window I noticed how gaunt my face had become. I hadn't eaten a meal in days and my body, requiring some kind of sustenance, had started to feed itself. My clothes, weighed down by the rain, stretched my frame so I looked over six feet tall. My usually well-groomed hair looked neglected and my eyes had become withdrawn.

We had broken up just days before, or had we? Truth be told, I can't remember what my interpretation of our relationship status was. Through the phone I heard her say she missed dancing with me in the kitchen to stupid songs. The comment ran off me like the water on the café window. I instinctively walked towards the door, and as I raised my hand to push it I noticed the sign reading closed. My hand seemed out of the loop and went ahead with the push and I immediately realised my mistake.

"Sorry, forgot you were closed."

A man with his back to and nearest the door stood up and replied.

"No worries. You look soaked, would you like a drink? Don't mind us." It struck me as odd that a proprietor – I wasn't sure if he was, but he spoke with the air of one – would suggest to a potential customer, 'don't mind us'. I winced at the thought of being the only patron in a quiet café and having such a personal conversation. I didn't want to pour my feelings over the canvas of my body for the world to examine and laugh at like some abstract painting. In reply to my own thoughts I said 'better not', and promptly left the premises. What a stupid thing to say! Better not – I might catch food poisoning? Better not – I might enjoy it? What must he have thought?

I caught up with her one-sided conversation and conceded I had missed her questions about who I was talking to and whether I was listening to her. She hung up, and there I was on the pavement, wet and dripping as if covered in paint.

Our problems had started a few days before that. She had seemed preoccupied and had got less and less talkative. Every evening it became harder to engage her in conversation. I wondered if she was generally dispirited, if I had done something in particular, or maybe there was something larger that was stressing her. I asked her about it. She paused a few moments on the sofa, which felt like waiting on the number 29 in rush hour, eventually managing a sentence.

"I'm not sure if I love you anymore."

I began shivering on our fraying carpet. My sympathetic nervous system kicked into action, overdrive in fact, and I started to feel uncomfortably numb.

The following days were like a clumsy soap opera story. We tried separate bedrooms – she moved in with a friend when that failed. We met twice on neutral ground to talk and she proclaimed she wanted to be with me, but at the same time needed to be sure before making any decisions. She also stated she was utterly abashed and didn't know what she wanted. It amazed me it took her so long to work this out.

She continued on at work, and each night she went clubbing or drinking with friends. I was without details of her actions, but this seemed bizarrely outgoing behaviour for someone in turmoil. I had spent each night on the carpet in the company of bottles of wine, tugging the frays. I had taken some swiftly arranged holiday at work, and had not seen or spoken to any family or friends. My pride had taken such a drubbing, I was unwilling to speak to anyone about it. Embarrassment consumed me when I imagined telling someone.

God, what a vacant life I led! It made me realise it had been pretty barren for a while. I came home from work, and waited for her. I rarely saw friends as Kate didn't get on with most of them. After nine hours at work, I didn't want to go out in the city drinking with her friends. On Wednesdays, my day off, I usually bought some fresh food, cooked a favourable lunch, sat down armed with some new DVDs and a bottle of red, and fell asleep. Sundays were similar only with Kate in attendance, and more foreign language DVDs. I had no hobbies, few friends, did no sports, played no instruments. What had happened to my life?

And then suddenly I had no Kate, the only thing I looked forward to in the day. The thing I returned home to, spent my Sundays and evenings with, and routinely fell asleep on.

At least, I thought I had no Kate. She continued to call to try and arrange a meeting, but after hearing about her burgeoning social life and feeling pity at my withered one, I refused. I said I needed some distance. I don't know why I said that; I had the distance from Finsbury Park to Camden and plenty of time to think about things without work distracting me. And yet I could not focus, could not order my thoughts. She called every day, each time suggesting a meet in increasingly diplomatic language. Then, having stumbled upon the ultimate way to breach my defences, she said she was worried about me – I stopped fighting. The uncertainty was eating away at me and when she asked if she should come to Finsbury Park, I replied I would meet her in Camden. She asked where we should go and it just came out.

"The Kennedys", I said. "Where? It's just off the High Street, round the corner from M&S."

"Why not just meet at the Bean Cup?" That had been our regular haunt and was in fact, opposite M&S.

"I think it would be better to go somewhere neutral," My mind started to wander again. It happens to me a lot during stressful conversations. "Sorry, what did you say?"

"I said, what do you mean neutral ground? We both go to the Bean Cup, and as far as I know, neither of us holds shares in the place", she said.

I instantly got on my high horse. As I looked down at her, all I could come up with was; "Look, do you want to discuss where we meet, or actually meet? Besides, just 'cos I happen to pick somewhere..."

"All right, we can meet at The Kennedys. I will find it. Is three o'clock suitable?"

"Perfect", I replied. It gave me four hours before we met. How could a time to meet and finalise the end of a relationship be perfect? I mean, you wouldn't say that if it was your life on the line would you?

'What time would you like to be electrocuted sir, 10.30 suit?'

'Yes, that would be perfect, ta.'

Chapter 2

So, I found myself outside the café again, six days after my first brief visit. I thought I would go early to scout the place out. I wanted her to think it was a common retreat of mine, so the least I should be able to do was tell her where the toilets were and which special café lattes they had. She always drank them, but I can't see the point. I mean it's coffee – the drink is coffee, and these days people stray further and further from the base form. First it's milk, then it's warm milk, then it's frothy milk, then it's sugar, caramel syrup, cinnamon, fucking chocolate bits, bread and jam. When will it end?

At three in the afternoon most cafés in Camden are besieged, and so unlike at the Bean Cup where they know us, I thought I would be able to sip my black sugarless coffee in anonymity.

"Welcome back. You want to risk a drink this time?" said the proprietor with a grin. So much for anonymity.

"Yeah, sorry about that, I didn't mean, I mean I thought there was, um something wrong with the place. That's not what I thought, but I was on the phone to someone and they wanted a err private conversation."

"Well, I'm not normally in the habit of eavesdropping on people's conversations. Doesn't go down well with customers."

The impending meeting with Kate was nibbling at my insides. I felt really nervous and I could only manage a half-smile, half-frown whilst staring hollow at him.

"You all right?" he said.

"Sorry. I guess, um, well..." I couldn't help but consider if I should pour out my heart to him. I felt vulnerably submissive.

"Coffee?"

"Yeah, coffee." I said.

"Black, white?"

"Black."

"Strong, medium?"

"Strong."

"Syrup?"

"Syrup." I wasn't sure whether if being hypnotised felt like this.

"I got you there. We don't do syrup. That's for the fancy places. I just asked because you looked like you might be the type." He said this bereft of sarcasm.

I could have been offended by the 'look like the type' remark had I had time to dwell on it, but instead she chose this time to enter the café. Shit, she was early as well. I had had no time to scout the place. Instead, I had managed to establish that I had the personality of a parrot and was unable to string together ten words without 'err', 'um' or 'I mean'. I had also failed to find out where the toilets were.

"Hello", she said, too jolly for my liking.

"Where are the toilets?"

"I sure hope that's not because of me?" She was trying to offer it as an ice-breaker. Instead it was more like a chainsaw through my self-esteem, which at that moment had the consistency of jelly.

"No, I just wondered, in case you needed them."

"How considerate! I'm fine for the moment though, thank you."

She turned to the proprietor.

"What flavour lattes do you have?"

"Coffee."

"Oh," she said, "well a 'coffee' latte please."

"Coming up, and there's yours. It needs four minutes brewing." He pushed a tray towards me with a cafetiére, and a cup and saucer on it. "Are you together?"

"That's kind of what we're here to discuss." I said. Good, at last, I was starting to make some sense and claw back some jelly.

"I meant for paying, are you together or separate, but if you want some privacy then I can manage that too." She giggled and I blushed.

I felt like finding that toilet and flushing my head down it for making myself look so dim, only I still didn't know where it was.

"Where are you from?" I asked him.

"England", he accompanied this with a jesting beam, awaiting the next question.

"OK, I'll just grab a table."

I trudged over to the window and sat down. It was one of only two tables on the same side of the café as the counter. I didn't want neighbouring tables listening in and it was the furthest place from anyone else I could sit.

You never sit down next to anyone unless you can't help it. It would be like going on a date with a woman, and when you both agree on a table in the pub, sitting on her lap. And on public transport, you always sit at least two seats away from someone: there must always be a free seat between you and others. When you cannot sit two seats away from someone, you have to ensconce yourself on the seat in front of or behind the person. That's acceptable because you are still giving them personal space. What happens when all the seats are taken? Then it is down to personality. At least now you have permission to sit next to a person, though I prefer to stand.

Once, I was on the receiving end of a prank on a bus. I was travelling to Stratford and was the only person on the upper deck when two lads got on. One sat next to me, the other on the seat in front of me. At first I thought they were trying to mug me and my mind conjured up scenarios that left me on the back seat without money, trousers or bus ticket, but after two minutes of snickering it dawned on me it was their idea of fun. It didn't stop me worrying that at some point they might jump me though. When I could take it no more and planned to get off the bus – six stops early – I stood up and they fled, laughing grotesquely. Bastards!

The aroma of freshly ground coffee roused my senses and I absorbed the café. It had pastel shades of yellow, orange, and blue, and a full window entrance bathing the place in natural light. The floor and furniture were wooden, and on the walls hung some modern art 'colour' paintings. Abstract some call them, colour charts to me. The counter extended the wooden theme with a glass display boasting home-made cakes. There were seven adequate tables and two higher wall tables at the rear. The back wall led to the other exits, three doors. One of these, I deduced, must be the toilet – well done Sherlock.

A few moments later Kate came over with her café latte and a slice of some biscuit base cake with a ridiculous amount of cream on it. I suddenly felt wretched and serious.

"They have some gorgeous looking cakes here."

"U huh" I reluctantly agreed, annoyed at the small talk.

"Have you been here many times? It seems a quaint place, he's very friendly", she said.

A pang of jealousy registered somewhere around my stomach, which had not been fed since last night. I so wanted to have a regular conversation with her, but anger won through.

"Look, I appreciate the effort, but you wanted to see me, and here I am. What did you want?"

She sighed before taking a long pause. I think she felt that I would prompt her, but I decided to sit this one out. The hardest thing about this whole situation was the helplessness. She stared at her café latte with her head cocked to one side for over sixty seconds, looked up as if someone had prodded her in the back and just blurted it out.

"I miss you. I miss spending time with you. I miss coming home to your cooking on Wednesdays. I miss dancing in the kitchen with you...I'm just not sure I love you." She wriggled with something else to offer, but it didn't come to fruition.

A man in a motorised wheelchair travelled past the window very slowly. He drove right next to us, and despite the severity of the conversation, all I could concentrate on was the man. He was painfully slow. Do they have varying speeds on wheelchairs? Are there Ferraris and Skodas in the wheelchair world?

"What are you saying then?" I snapped back to our conversation. Self-pity prevented me from telling her how I really felt. I realised she was probably looking for something from me, but at the time, I was smothered in a me-first attitude.

"Nothing...especially. I'm still unclear what I want, but I want you to know I miss you." There was another long pause as I was looking everywhere but at her. The proprietor, meticulously cleaning out the coffee machine, had given us a wide berth.

"Have you seen Kim?" she said.

Kim, my best friend, lives in Croydon, and this was the reason I told myself I hadn't seen him for three months. It takes so long to get from north to south London, or east to west, that he might as well live in Birmingham.

"No."

"Why?"

"I don't really want the pity. The uncomfortable silences. I don't want him feeling bad, searching for what to say. Besides, he has plenty of shit going on in his life."

"I am sure he would want to know. He is your friend. You would want him to call you if..." she didn't finish the sentence, she didn't have to.

"I guess I am also embarrassed." Slimy tears gathered at the back of my throat and formed a lump, which I swallowed. I looked away again, took in a large breath and forced it out.

So there you have it. It was another unproductive meeting. Nothing was resolved. I half expected it to be an official break up talk; but she felt the same as before, clueless; and I felt the same as before, helpless. She complained I didn't show enough emotion, that I didn't cry, or tell her what I wanted. I tried to point out it's illogical to tell someone what you want when you are not calling all the shots and it's hard to show emotions when the ones you have are so bruised and battered, you don't recognise them. She said that logic shouldn't come into this type of situation and I suppose she had a point. I didn't want to agree with her, though.

"Listen, I can collect the rest of my stuff on Saturday, while you are at work", she said.

"I'm not working Saturday, I'm on holiday."

"Oh right, I forgot. Well, if you could let me know if you are going to be out of the house for a while, I could do it then."

"Why do you want me out of the house?" My responses were gaining momentum.

"I just thought it would be easier."

"How are you moving your stuff? You can't carry your TV on the bus."

"I can find someone to help me out."

"But Jane hasn't got a car. Nor Carol."

"Well, I have another friend with a car."

I felt like a dog with a bone now. Anything to avoid me facing the real situation.

"Would the reason you are being so evasive have anything to do with the person being a guy?"

She sighed again. It seemed more through annoyance at the conversation than me finding out.

"Yes, but...he's merely a friend. A man I met." Her use of the word 'man' made me feel like a boy and I sat upright, like a hyperactive pupil ready to provoke the teacher.

"Where did you meet him?"

"What is this, twenty questions?"

"If it is, I still have another fifteen or so. Is he the reason you split up with me? Having difficulty telling me were you?" With each new sentence my voice was getting louder and I hated that. I hate losing control. I held myself back. "Are you seeing him?"

"Yes, in an hour as a matter of fact."

"Well, you don't waste time. Don't let me keep you, please." I was aware that the proprietor had suddenly taken an interest in the conversation. He was being very discreet, but seemed to be surveying the effect our discussion was having on the other customers: a girl in a wheelchair with a friend, a guy in his eighties, and what looked like a couple of Scandinavian hikers preparing to tackle Snowden.

"Nothing is happening between us, he is purely a friend. And he is very easy to talk to."

"So is a vegetable." I realised whatever high ground I was on had quickly turned into a swamp and I was sinking.

"All right! He is interested in me. But I told him in no uncertain terms I was not interested. My head is lacking clarity at the moment and he knows exactly what the situation is with me and you."

"Nice! Can I meet him? Maybe he can tell *me* what the fuck is going on."

"I meant, I was honest with him and told him all about us."

"So what happens in an hour? Will he give it the old – 'How was it? You poor thing! Come here for a hug' routine?" At the very least, I was in the swamp up to my hips now.

"He has not tried anything on with me. He has been very respectful, and is just supporting me."

"What with?"

It seemed like the proprietor had been gearing up for a subtle cough, but the end came without his assistance. Kate remained calm and wisely ignored my question.

"Here is what we will do. We will come round on Saturday at two o'clock. I will leave it up to you whether you are there. I will let myself in. I promise I will only take what is mine and then I will post the keys through the letterbox. Is that acceptable?"

I was back to staring out the window at a pigeon, imagining how much simpler life was for him. I thought of how my friend Miles would have a different opinion. He once scared some German woman off at uni after cornering her at a party. He drunkenly confessed his belief that being cruel to pigeons demoted humans to the status of Nazis. In his definition of cruel, he included walking through a group of them, thus forcing them to fly away. He didn't stop there. He enquired aggressively as to how she would feel if a giant pigeon fifty times the size of her, came and walked through the middle of the party forcing them all to flee. He even started to imitate what this might look like, making himself bigger and waving his hands wildly. At this point, the girl flew into some other guy's arms, who she ended up marrying and moving to Portsmouth with.

"Is that acceptable?" she prompted again.

"Yes." I felt like a deflated balloon. I sat there as she walked out, but my eyes couldn't even follow her. They were still fixed on the pigeon. Then suddenly it flew away to its freedom, its friends, its other life, or possibly to terrorise some humans at Trafalgar Square.

Chapter 3

The next day I was at a loss. The last thing I wanted was to mope around the flat and I was desperate for some fresh air, so I left with no fixed destination. After instinctively jumping on the first bus to come my way, I found myself in Camden once again. The Kennedys, I thought, was as good a place as any to head for. It was then I decided upon my goal for the day – to find out the proprietor's name.

"Paul, and yours?"

"Craig. Err, sorry about yesterday. I appreciate it's the last thing you want, an argument in the middle of your café scaring away your customers."

"No worries. You would be surprised how many of those conversations I witness. Not that I don't sympathise, but I am getting used to looking the other way. I take it things didn't really go the way you planned?"

"What makes you say that?"

"I would have thought if things turned out positively you would either be at work or with her." It was a terse observation and put me on the defensive.

Grey strands in thinning ginger hair betrayed his youthful buoyancy and revealed his forty something years more than any wrinkles could. My neck was a little stressed by having to look up to him, so I gave it a rest and scanned the place to see if any of yesterday's customers had returned. There were half a dozen new customers scattered around and the girl in the wheelchair was at the table opposite the counter with a man. She was rocking back and forth and making some high pitched squeals as well as the odd raspberry with her tongue. I couldn't help but feel this was directed at me. Paul noticed she had drawn my attention.

"She loves this song."

I recognised it from somewhere in the mid-90s. A song called Tax-Loss. I couldn't help but impart on him my musical knowledge.

"Big fan of Mansun is she?"

"Is that who it is? Well, if it's loud, she loves it. Don't you Donna?"

She craned her head round in the direction of the counter. She looked like a turtle slowly projecting its head out of its body to see if the rain has stopped. She made a low pitched hum and shook a tissue with her left hand, as if by way of approval, then proceeded to rock back and forth, furiously.

"Does she come here a lot?"

"Yeah. Donna lives round the corner and often comes here for coffee, don't you sweety?" Out came the turtle again. "Matt is one of her carers." I looked and saw the man soaking up a pool of spilt coffee from the table, a product of her 'dancing'.

"Oh, so er, she er, you um. Does she live alone?" I hadn't got a clue when it came to disabled people.

"No, she lives with five others." Paul buried himself in a cupboard under the cake display. Matt took over, offering his hand.

"All right, geezer."

"So are they all friends, or did they...." Paul popped back up and they both stared at me, quickly realising they would have to do the work.

"Nah, it's a social services group home. Like a care in the community package. Donna and the others all need 24-hour care."

"And Donna here thinks I make the best coffee in London", added Paul.

I thought it was about time that I spoke to Donna as I was the only one who hadn't yet.

"So, what makes it so good Donna? Donna?"

The turtle stared at me through her nearest eye. She looked like she was clocking me through a spyhole. I realised I was unlikely to receive an answer and felt like a parent asking its baby to explain the rules of baseball. Her black spiky hair fell off in all directions like a chive plant and her bottom lip looked swollen and drooped down a little. Her clothes seemed severely oversized, but I suspected she was very skinny underneath.

Paul sensed my diffident expression and asked me what I wanted to drink. As I ordered my black coffee, behind me I heard the squeak of the wheelchair becoming more and more violent.

"Was the dark roast all right yesterday? Do you like stronger coffee?"

"Yeah it was great. Not at all bitter."

"That's what I like to hear. In case you crave variety, we have five different roasts, ranging from light to dark, so if you ever fancy a change..."

"Same again, please."

The way he glided around his small kitchen area belied the amount of work that must be involved in running a café. The absence of sweat on his exposed skin could have been because of his casual linen clothing or his efficient prioritisation of tasks. I paid for the drink and sat at the scene of the previous day's crime by the window. Paul shouted after me whilst pointing to a door.

"In case you were wondering, the toilet is back there."

I started to think of what I was going to do. I felt dispirited at the lack of things I had to do, yet this could just as easily be positive – no ties, no loyalties. Although I could not take my mind off Kate, I couldn't describe my feelings as sadness. It felt more like self-pity, as if I was just pissed off at being treated unfairly by another human being. Or maybe I was just using that as an excuse to try and avoid thinking about her. A high pitch wail emanated from Donna and marked the change in music to a dance tune. I have little or no knowledge of dance music.

I began to feel guilty, thinking about what kind of life Donna led. She couldn't exactly choose to do what she wanted in the day. Her whole life was in the hands of others. From what I had seen, she could not speak or express her emotions, thoughts, or requests. On top of which, she was an obvious spectacle. Anyone in this café could not help but focus upon her, affording her no privacy. Without free will, without a choice, what kind of life was it? It was a life that a carer – whose compassion was arbitrary – chooses for her on the basis of what they think she might like. Or worse still, the carer might choose what she does on the basis of what would make life easiest for them. And she looked such a mess! Dribbling, waving a tissue around and screaming primordially. I began to feel a little better about my situation. Then I felt like a complete arsehole for writing off someone else's life.

Chapter 4

I was back again. Three times in three days. Paul seemed genuinely happy to see me, asking me how I was. I asked what he did with his life before he opened the café.

"I used to look after Donna. I was one of her carers, like Matt, but then I set up this place."

"On your own?"

"I had a friend who put some money in, but he didn't want to run it, just be a silent partner."

"Do you have any other people work here?"

"I have one guy who works here and the odd friend who helps out occasionally. Somebody has just left. Funnily enough, I am looking for someone to take over from him. You interested?"

"Me, God no. I mean – not God, just no. Well, I would be interested, but I have another job." I noticed there were only a couple of people in today and wondered how he managed to maintain a profitable business; Camden was expensive. "How do you do for customers? I mean, you're not on the high street here and it seems a little quiet here."

"I have many orders for take out. I make sandwiches in the mornings, mainly for business workers on the high street. This is only part of the building and not linked to the flats above, so it's quite cheap to rent. But it's getting too much work with the food as well. I had someone come in this morning for an interview, but she was kind enough to tell me she was only around for another six weeks before leaving, so that's no good. I have another one, she should be here now actually. Want to sit in on the interview?"

I laughed until I realised he was waiting for an answer.

"Me. You serious? I mean no thanks, but..."

"You are one of my regulars now, so you have a vested interest."

My heart suddenly warmed. I felt an odd sense of belonging that had been absent for a long time. His smile suggested it was no formal arrangement, but it still felt nice.

"What makes you think I'll be back here again?"

"You can help pick the person who serves you. How many other cafés offer that?" I noticed that Donna was not here today. The eighty-year old and the Scandinavians were also absent. Could I be the only possible regular?

A petite curly-haired girl burst through the door. She seemed out of breath and headed directly for Paul behind the counter. Her gait was wide and she appeared to skip between steps.

"I am Marie-Louise. Sorry if I 'ave kept you waiting. The traffic is really bad this afternoon and I was stuck in a bus."

"No, not at all. What would you like to drink?"

"Oh no, I am fine thank you."

"Nonsense, I insist. You turn up for an interview, the least I can do is offer you a drink, but you do have to make it."

I noticed that she was not English – French or Belgian I would say. I loved the way she dropped her Hs when she spoke. She wore a black, three-quarter length coat, black jeans, and her waterfall brown hair was tied back in a pony tail. She also had an extremely long scarf – thick, woollen, and yellow. It could have doubled as a hammock.

"OK, I will have a water", she said with a wide smile on her face. "And I think you will still want me to make a drink so how about this gentleman here?"

I was about to turn round until I realised I was the gentleman. I looked at Paul for approval and realised then I was unwittingly part of the 'interview'. The playful part of me wanted to give her a test, some elaborate concoction. Or see if her milk foaming skills were up to scratch with a cappuccino. Realising I didn't like these drinks, I ordered my boring black coffee.

"Ah, a purist", she offered.

I looked at Paul and noticed he was using this as entertainment. A chance to see how she would interact and test her drink-making skills at the same time. Paul showed her where everything was and told her which roast to use.

"I am more used to making espressos", she said apologetically.

Coffee making is an art form that the vast majority of purveyors completely fail to master. In fact they do worse than that: they butcher it. The best thing about having a good quality coffee is that it is part of a process. If you order a coffee and thirty seconds later are walking on the street coffee in hand, then the process has been by-passed and you might as well be drinking dirt water, which is often not far from the actuality.

Although it's enjoyed in many forms; with sugars, syrups, milk or cream, for me, anything added is just one more step away from the process. One more level of dilution in an already adulterated practice. The fact that Paul used freshly ground beans in various roasts, meant that he offered a choice in the taste of coffee. It's amazing how the country of origin, or roast can result in such differing tastes. I was a stickler for good coffee, and I must say Paul did serve good coffee.

"Tell us a bit about yourself. Forget the 'why you want a job' part. Tell us about you." Her smile seemed to sparkle as he said this and she chuckled.

"I come from Amboise in France." I was paying little attention to her words and lots of attention to her accent. French must be the sexiest non-native accent for spoken English. "I moved to Paris when I was nineteen to study Economics. Boring I know, but I thought it was a safe option. I think I managed to tire myself of Paris, or economics, I don't know. You know when you tend to link two things in your mind and no matter how hard you try you always make this subconscious link and so you are doomed? I think that is me and Paris. When I think of Paris, all I think of is micro- and macro-economics."

"What brought you across the Channel?"

"I finished my course last year and I came to London with my boyfriend. I needed a change and I wanted to live abroad and improve my English and England is so...so...charming."

I suddenly realised how I had already proposed, married, had two children; Jean-Paul and Celine; had a lovely cottage adjacent to some vineyard and she wrote articles for economics periodicals. We had a cat, and every day was an endless late Sunday afternoon, with long shadows and cool breezes and I...I...I?

I decided to concentrate more on what she was saying like England is charming. Charming is a word that is underused by English people. Ironic given that it is commonly used to describe us and our country. Charm for me has the negative connotation of a smug bastard who wants to screw some poor romantic girl, and then leave while she is asleep and go back to his wife and kids. I smiled and hoped she wasn't telepathic.

"What is so funny?"

"Nothing!"

"Was my English wrong? I said something wrong, no?"

"No, I just like the fact that the only people who think England is charming are people who aren't from England."

"You don't think it is charming?"

I thought about it for a moment. This was not how the interview was supposed to go. How did the interviewee get the upper hand? She was supposed to sit there, feel nervous and agree with me. I looked at Paul and realised I was the only one who still felt this was an interview. To them it was now just a nice discussion.

Although I didn't like being put on the spot, I kind of liked the attention. It's a much underrated compliment, being asked what you think.

"I think it's natural for everyone to slag off where they live. It's human nature to never be satisfied: It's cold? We moan it's freezing; When it warms up? We moan it's too hot; We moan it rains and then when it stops, we say we need more rain; When we live in a shit hole we moan, and then when we are surrounded by beauty we focus on the shit details."

Despite being a hastily erected musing, I meant it. Granted, it was not the deepest observation of my life, but I think it got me out of a hole.

"I think I know what you mean. When I lived in Paris, I lived in the most amazing apartment and it was a beautiful walk to university every day through historic areas with aged buildings. But all I could see was the dirt and the people living on the streets and the lifeless new shops. Then a friend came and stayed with me. After taking her to the obvious places, I asked if there was anything she wanted to do and she said 'no, just walk around'. Just walk around! That made her happy! When I asked her what she wanted to see, she replied that she wanted to breathe in Paris. To try and get the feel of what it would be like to live there, as if she led a different life. She said she always enjoyed imagining what it would be like to live somewhere far better than actually living there."

I was surprised by how passionately she had responded.

"Did I say something wrong?"

"No. I was just thinking about what you said. About missing things, or missing out on things. Sometimes I feel like I reside here, but don't live here."

"Do you like London?"

I glanced at Paul, who looked like he was watching a particularly juicy episode of Jerry Springer.

"Not really, no."

"Why are you living here?"

It was a good question, and one I felt I should be tackling on my own. Instead, I was having my life analysed on Kennedys' TV.

"Well, I am probably leaving, but haven't made any firm plans yet".

Was I? Where was I going? My God! I had been on the rocks with Kate for two weeks and already I had lost the ability to converse with normal humans without digging holes for myself. Who was I trying to impress that I could not give them straight answers? Still, surely talking this stuff over with someone was positive. At least I cared about what they thought of me enough, to tell them what I thought they wanted to hear in order for them to like me. I had figured that much out – next I just needed to stop it and grow a backbone.

"Enough about me. You are the one supposed to be on trial here, tell us some more?" I was talking as if the place belonged to Paul and me!

"I 'ad a few jobs in England. I taught French. I was a guide for a French holiday firm, or at least tried to be. I read up on all the history to wow them with facts, but all they ever wanted was to stare at 10 Downing Street, Buckingham Palace and the Houses of Parliament and they seemed happy. Not that there is anything wrong with that, but I was giving too many facts and not enough entertainment. So I travelled around for a few weeks, then came back and worked in a bar near Hyde Park and that was just shit." Something about the way she pronounced 'shit' made it sound less like a swear word and more like some grievous bodily offence visited on her by the pub. "And now I need a new job."

"So when are you available from?"

"I can work whatever days you need, but..."; she stopped mid-sentence.

"Go on."

"Well, is this a part-time or full-time job?"

"I can offer 30 hours. Five days. The shifts are 7 till 1.30 or 12 till 6.30. We can usually work earlies and lates around appointments."

"That would be fine. I mean, if you offered me the job." She turned to me. "Are you going to try the coffee?"

"Huh? Oh yeah." I noticed that she had already placed my cafetiére in front of me. Presumably at the time I was planning to move to the south of France with her. Now that all eyes were on me, Paul weighed in.

"This is the moment of truth. If the coffee is given the thumbs up by my chief taster here, then you have a job. If not, I'm afraid it's back to the pub for you."

I remained silent presuming he had already made his decision. It was hardly the stereotypical interview. I acted up for the occasion. I poured a small amount out into the cup, lifted it to my nose and smelt it, inhaling the fresh aroma through closed eyes. I took the first sip, careful not to dwell on the front of the tongue for fear of burning it. I drank it down, pursed my lips and moved them to the side as though giving careful consideration. Marie-Louise began to chuckle. I began to nod my head and as they anticipated my final speech, I smiled. "It's perfect. Thank you. How much do I owe you?"

"Oh no. Please, let me buy this for you. I would like to buy my first customer a drink."

"Forget the money for now." Paul said. "If you want the job it's yours. You don't have to tell me right now, but I need to know by the end of the day."

"Well, thank you. I mean, that would be great. I am sure I will take it, but I just want to check first about the money situation. Um, is it rude to ask about what the pay would be?"

"Forgive me, I'll give you some privacy to talk about details. And thank you once again for the coffee." I married my cup with its saucer again, and tray in hand headed for what was going to be my contemplation spot for the third day in a row.

They smiled in appreciation and took up residence at a table. So what was she going to check? Obviously with the boyfriend. I was about to moan about how all the good girls were taken when I reminded myself about my somewhat less than ideal situation. After all, did I not feel anything for Kate? Was I not missing her? It had been nearly two years and that's a big commitment. And she hadn't even moved out yet. What would I do if she changed her mind?

But on the other hand, I had had my bubble burst in the last couple of weeks. I had spread my misery over all the places I had visited since then, and if I was looking for a little self-esteem boost, so what? Was I so wrong to seek a little attention from an attractive female? Nothing had happened, or was going to happen. I wasn't actively pursuing her, I just wanted someone to be nice to me. Someone who might see a little good in me, so I could see the same thing and feel a little better about myself again – albeit for an hour or two.

I looked over and saw Paul and Marie-Louise laughing. She seemed to be quite taken with him and for the second time in three days, I felt a bit jealous of a female showing him attention. I sat there wallowing in self-pity and lost track of time. A little time later, Marie-Louise walked by cheerily.

"Bye Craig, it was nice meeting you." I looked up and smiled, hopefully in time. I was left staring at the point on the pavement that she first stepped on after leaving the café. I focused on that point and it was a real effort to snap out of the moment. It's soothing to look in soft focus at one spot. It almost puts me on standby – unable to register or respond to anything, except a direct question.

"Now are you going to be a regular? She should be the person to serve you coffee from now on, or me." Paul sat down opposite me looking like a cross between a Samaritan and a McDonald's employee: eager to help, and help quick.

I focused again on his broad grin. I looked down at my coffee, picked up my untouched spoon and looked at my reflection in it. I was smiling.

"Yeah, I guess I can manage that."

Chapter 5

I suppose it was inevitable where I would spend my Saturday, or at least a part of it. I didn't want to be in the flat when Kate turned up with her friend. I didn't want to give *him* the satisfaction of being the nice guy. I was sure I could do nothing to avoid acting like a loveless arsehole. In addition to this, he would get to see where we live, or rather had lived together. No matter how much I rearranged furniture, tidied up mess, hung new pictures, or scrubbed the stains off the fridge door, it would still give away clues as to what our life was like together, and the last thing I wanted to do was to give this guy a footsie to her heart.

Instead, I tried to kid myself. 'I suppose I could try and fit her in, but it is just too tight a squeeze' – this was the sort of self-denial that occupied my brain all Saturday morning.

I had rung Kim the night before. He had recently completed his thesis for his doctoral degree entitled: The influence of indigenous religious ideologies on gender relations in Mali. He was still studying though, as he had an oral test to complete before he was finished. His father had refused to fund him for the previous six months since Kim announced that after completion of his degree, he wanted to go and live in a mud hut in the Sahara to do more research – Kim's dad wanted him to work in his museum in Brighton.

Other than that, he said things were generally good. I avoided small talk as I knew this would lead onto Kate and it felt too raw to talk about that on the phone. Besides, I didn't want him to meet up with me simply because he thought he should. He said he was busy on Saturday and had plans with his girlfriend, who he said he had been neglecting of late. Sensing the reciprocal question about my girlfriend I quickly offered another day – Monday, one o'clock? He agreed and I gave him directions to The Kennedys. As soon as I put the phone down, I realised there was a problem with Monday: work. I decided that was something I could think over during my hours avoiding Kate on Saturday afternoon.

I arrived just after one and the place was rammed. I had barely seen it half-full in my visits. All the tables were full and only one of the high chairs at the back was free. A woman in her sixties with a fur coat, over-generous make-up and three starch-stiff paper bags full of designer clothes, was exiting. Hardly a regular Kennedys' customer I thought.

"Have a good one Mrs. Hawley. Take care of yourself", Paul said to her. It felt as if the café was rooting out my prejudices.

There were two people before me in the queue. One guy was readying to carry his drinks away, the other was a woman trying to accommodate the wishes of her friend on the other side of the café with do-it-yourself sign language. She looked more like a football manager communicating a change in tactics from the sideline and all her signs were accompanied by exaggerated mouthing of the words. The signs included shaking her cupped hand in a downward motion to ask if she wanted cocoa powder on her hot chocolate; and transferring cream from an imaginary pot, with an imaginary spoon, onto an imaginary chocolate cake that looked deadly to the hips.

Another guy was making the drinks with Paul. He must have been nearly six foot six, extremely dark skinned and clean shaven on his head, which was perfectly round. Paul looked up.

"Hi Craig. French roast is it?" He was friendly, but I felt more like one of the many instead of one of the few. Still, what right had I to preferential treatment? I had only begun to come here in the last week, spill my life out onto to his nice, clean tables and drink free coffee. Well, once anyway.

"Yeah, black. And, a slice of the coffee and walnut cake please Paul, thank you."

I had to get the 'Paul' in so listeners would think I was a regular! Trying to win compliments with bribes and sweet talk: it was like living with Kate again.

I placed my empty coat and bag on the vacant chair. It was facing the back wall which had a huge mirror on it, giving the illusion of greater space. When I turned back to the counter I realised, having looked at the whole café without the mirror for the first time, it was really quite small. There were at least twenty people and the various conversations mingled and competed with each other as if it were a PTA meeting. There were already two more people ordering drinks. My drink and cake were waiting for me and I paid Paul.

"How are you today?" he said distractedly.

"So, so" I replied. It was not the time and place to start anything in depth. "Actually, I'm quite good."

"That's good to hear. Sorry I can't talk, but we are rushed here. Maybe chat later, OK?"

"No problem. I can see you..." He was already taking an order. The guy making drinks looked over at me and offered me a smile while frothing milk. I wasn't sure if he was laughing at me or being sympathetic. I took my prizes and mooched back to my chair.

I had some blank paper in my pocket and a pen and decided to start planning. First up, what was I going to do in the next week? I always used to do this when I had a full social calender and I was in danger of missing appointments or double booking. Since I began seeing Kate though, the holes in my calender had increased in size and number. Double bookings were a thing of the past and even single bookings seldom occurred. So, I had decided I needed to write down and plan a week that kept me busy. It didn't necessarily need people in it, but things; things I wanted to do, and things I needed to do.

I halved my paper three times to give me eight sections and scribbled in the days, spanning from the coming, to the following Monday. First, I filled in my working hours of 9-6 every day except Wednesday and Sunday. This occupied many of the anxiety-inducing blanks.

I am an electrical product salesman. This basically involves talking to people and trying to convince them to buy: more expensive products than they need; additional products they don't want; insurance for the product they can't afford; and when they phone up with questions for help with the product post-purchase, failing to give them the assistance they actually require. I am quite good at it as well. By good, I mean I always reach my sales targets – the company's way of measuring if I am good. If you have the right approach, customers often take every word you say like stardust and follow you round the store as if you're the pied piper. Half of 'the right approach' is about high confidence and low scruples. I found this very difficult when I first started the job, although I learnt to adapt over time until it became an intuitive process. The adaptation was, I admit, more for survival than by any desire to achieve. I was paid on commission and so the more I sold, the more money I made, and the cost of living in London means you always need more money.

Everything you say, you believe, and if you lie, you believe it is for their own good. Anyone who has an on/off switch for their emotions can be a decent salesman. People often talk about successful salesmen having the gift of the gab as if words alone sell things, but this is rubbish. I have made some outrageously dumb comments to sell things and it's luck, not judgement that makes people continuously nod their head in agreement. These comments have included:

◈ When confronted with a customer who wanted a table top fridge, but was bemused why they were so expensive, "You know what they say: half the size, twice the price!"

◈ When one man was unsure about spending fifty pounds extra on a new vacuum cleaner: "When the woman is happy in her housework, the man feels it in his stomach."

◇ And when someone questioned the necessity for better sound quality for his five-year-old son's birthday hi-fi: "Sound quality is food for the ears!"

It's a mistake to think that just because someone works in an electrical retail shop, they know everything about all the products. But why disappoint them, my manager says? People want to believe! The people come in instantly feeling inferior to you, and as long as you maintain that relationship, they'll buy what you want. Of course, you get some people who come in loaded with money, think you are shit and treat you like it. However, these people usually buy expensive products because their money gives them an excessive sense of superiority and because they think expensive is best, and so you are rewarded in commission for your servility. If you want to sell and take your morals to work, leave them in the staff room when you go out on the shop floor.

Recently however, it was getting harder to knit the wool to pull over people's eyes. The week after Kate dropped her bomb was my worst week of sales in over two years. One might think this was understandable, but it wasn't just because I felt shit. It was also because when confronted with simple questions such as, 'why do I need to spend the extra seventy pounds on this hi-fi?' I paused and replied, 'if I am totally honest, you don't need to'. *Don't need to? If I am totally honest?* My manager pulled me up in disbelief that a veteran salesman could make such a rookie mistake. He reminded me these were phrases that should never pass a salesman's lips. 'Need is only to be used in positive sentences', he said, 'and honesty doesn't exist'. Nevertheless, I continually found myself answering all the questions they asked me truthfully.

Next, I filled in my appointment with Kim on Monday at one o'clock. I had to decide what I was going to do about the Kim/work overlap. I toyed with my options. I could:

◈ phone in sick.

◈ appeal to my manager's better side by telling him the whole Kate story. Trouble is, his better side is hardly sunshine at the beach. It is at best, overcast with little prospect of sunshine.

◈ go and see my doctor.

◈ quit and find another job.

◈ quit and leave London.

◈ or I could go to work and cancel Kim.

I snapped out of my meditative musing when I heard a voice from my right.

"Excuse me?" It was an elderly lady. She was gesturing towards the sugar, which I was hypnotically spinning round. I passed it to her silently. She seemed pleased, yet apologetic: as if I was preparing to run the Olympic 100m sprint and she had just disturbed my concentration by asking for an autograph. She moved gingerly and slowly poured the sugar onto her spoon before stirring it into her tea.

"Sorry, I was in my own world."

"That's all right, dear." She spoke with her gaze fixed on her tea, stirring with total concentration.

"I..." she didn't look up. I noticed she had one of those awful chequered trolley bags that must be handed out free with your first pension because you never see anyone going to work with them. It was bereft of air and looked almost empty. I was at a loss for something to say. Still looking down at her tea, she filled the void.

"I only needed the sugar, dear." It seemed like such a pointless thing to say. Of course I knew that! Why did she tell me that? Did she think she had annoyed me? It almost sounded like an apology.

I swung back to my cake and separated a piece with my fork. The cream smeared my mouth with a sweet coffee taste and the walnuts texturised this beautifully. A sip of coffee washed all this down coating my throat. I felt revitalised.

"Sorry, I'll start again. I was just deep in thought and...it happens when I..." Back to basics, Craig. "Have you done much shopping?"

"Not much. I just needed a few things for the weekend."

"What did you buy?"

"Just some vegetables and soup."

"Have you finished your shopping?"

"Nearly" she said. I looked at her bag again and it was less than a quarter full. Talk about overkill.

"You don't seem to have bought much", she said as though responding to my thoughts.

"Yeah. I thought I needed some stuff, but...Do you live in Camden?"

"Not far. Just off Eversholt Street." I recognised the street name as being just a few streets away from customers' addresses I had taken at work.

"Are you from London?"

"Yes. I was born and bred in Muswell Hill." She looked up from her tea. "Bit different now to what it was."

"Really? I have only been through it on the bus."

"It's all bars and restaurants now. Lots of younger people and TV types. It's still quite nice, but far too expensive to live there."

"How long have you lived near here?"

"We moved to Somers Town not long after the war. It was quite different then. Always residential, but not such a mix of people. We had none of your Yugoslavians or Indians. It's a very mixed area now. You're not from London though are you?"

"No, I'm from Bristol." I skipped a beat as I prodded the memories of a life far removed.

"And what brought you to London?"

"Oh, I guess the city lights. I always liked big cities and, this is the one. Dead expensive though."

"You wouldn't believe the half of it. It wasn't always that way. You didn't need to be able to count in the old days, things were so cheap. I remember when coffee was just a few pence. All your everyday things weren't even ten pence: apples, lettuce, tomatoes, chocolate." I smirked with the uncomfortable realisation that I had just been roped into a conversation reminiscing about the past – I was trapped. I was mute, but sure my mouth was opening and closing like a goldfish. I realised my part in the conversation was to simply sit there, nod and be polite. "Our rent was about four pounds a week. Was it four pounds? Yes, about that. Today, we'd pay about a thousand pounds. It can't keep up like this. People just don't have the money."

"Well, we do earn a lot more money than before."

"Still – the price of a coffee!" She said this as if it was a clinching argument. I wish I knew what she meant.

"If you don't mind my asking, why do you come to this café? I mean, there are so many cafés in this area, many closer to you and…"

"More suitable for older people you mean?"

I squirmed. That was not what I meant, but I couldn't come up with an answer quick enough, and now it seemed like that was precisely what I meant.

"It's all right dear, no offence taken. We know Paul, so I came here a lot with my husband. He has passed away now, but my grand-daughter still comes in here. She loves the place."

I wondered if Paul and her grand-daughter have or had a thing. I didn't want to offend her though and felt it prudent to shut up. I had recently perfected the art of putting my foot in where it didn't fit. I looked up and couldn't see Paul. Marie-Louise wasn't around. I still didn't know for sure whether she had taken the job. Would her boyfriend let her work here? I really wanted to see her again, she was just...fresh. Something new and interesting in my life, which come to think of it the whole café was.

I was quite definitely a creature of habit. When faced with change, I am like a fish washed up on the beach? I struggle, can't get comfortable, and spend my whole time focusing on the future when things will hopefully be normal again. I think the only reason I can sell well is because I have done it for over seven years. When customers come into the shop, it's my domain. They put their trust in me and this feeds my self-confidence. But when I have to go to new places, I just can't do it. I would never have come to this place, had I not wanted to try and jazz up my mundane life to Kate. Paul was probably aware of the situation and allowed me to sit and wallow, and occasionally try and lift me out of it, but without Paul, without Marie-Louise, without Donna even, I felt once again like a fish out of water. The only difference was, I had an old lady for company and I suddenly felt very depressed.

My thoughts started to drift to the flat. I thought of what Kate might have removed already and what she still had to. A glance at my watch confirmed she would be there. I pictured *him* lounging on my couch, laughing at my pitiful taste and feeling very smug and superior. His legs stretched out onto the coffee table and arms extended on the backrest of the couch in a messianic pose. Then she comes in the room, reads his smirk and they start laughing together at how pathetic I am.

'What were you thinking?' he says in disbelief.

'I wasn't', she replies, declining her neck. Then she pounces on him and unpeels his shirt, all giggles and slander.

"I must be off now young man, but it was nice talking with you. Have a nice day." The old lady had risen, and with that she vanished. Well, it was a bit more dawdlingly and deliberate than that, but she upped and left.

"You too." I added. I didn't find out her name.

Chapter 6

Despite my efforts, my diary didn't get filled in for that week. I hadn't the physical or emotional energy to try out any new things. I left shortly after the lady, and when I got back to my flat, it was empty. Actually it was full, but there was so much stuff that I had forgotten did not belong to me, all I could focus on was what was missing. Her stamp on me was greater than I had calculated, and after she had removed the material imprint, I was left with a gaping hole. I felt sorry for myself the whole day.

After the wasted Sunday, Monday morning came and I had decided my course of action. I woke up and rang my boss. I was ill I said, migraines all over the weekend and I was going to the doctor's, assuming I could muster the energy to get there. He seemed mildly annoyed, but resigned to the fact there was little he could do about it.

After the doctor's I would go and meet Kim in The Kennedys. It was a bit close to work and therefore a little risky, but I knew nobody would venture down the side streets and my apathy led to me feeling indifferent about such a reckless action. As I was walking towards the café, it occurred to me that if Marie-Louise had taken the job, that Monday could be her first day. Adrenalin starting pumping and my mind started swimming in pre-constructed conversations. When I reached the street of The Kennedys, I saw Kim walking from the opposite direction. We offered each other a wave of recognition.

Kim looks a little like a Gothic super hero from a comic book. He is slim, with hard-to-place southern Asian looks and shoulder length shiny black hair that often makes women jealous. His slightly wider eyes and warm complexion make him seem somewhat exotic and despite the fact that he never quite looks like he fits in, his personality fits in everywhere. Very often he wears a long black suede trench coat with an intricate oriental pattern weaved into it. His clothes underneath are always skin tight and he has the physique of an athlete without an ounce of fat. This is explained by him living off a strict diet of four hours sleep, caffeine and little food.

Kim is my longest serving friend and I've known him since secondary school. We forged our friendship over a burette in a science lab. We had been forced together to continue an experiment we had begun the previous lesson with our partners. However, our partners were both sick and so we were put into a pair to finish the experiment. I had decided before that day that I didn't like him because he was incredibly smart, incredibly good looking and he knew it. We were in the middle of the experiment, in which we had to measure out some hydrochloric acid, and we had forgotten to close the stopcock at the bottom of the burette. We were carefully keeping an eye on the figures on the side so as not to use too much. We were perplexed as to why the level was not ascending when we noticed smoke rising before our eyes. The acid had gone straight through and was burning a hole in the laboratory floor. I think the hole is still there today.

When we met just outside The Kennedys, we hugged and mumbled clichés about the last time we saw each other and it being too long. As we turned to open the door I saw Marie-Louise immersed in cleaning the counter. I tried my best to act like I hadn't seen her. As we approached the counter she looked up and smiled broadly.

"Hello. 'Ow are you today?"

"Fine thanks, and you? Settling in well?"

"It's a little quiet now, but it was really busy this morning. Paul has just gone out to buy some rice milk. What can I get you both?"

"First, this is my friend Kim, and Kim this is Marie-Louise. She's new here." I cringed at sounding like I owned the place and was conducting a tour for potential customers. "I'll have a black coffee please, the French roast, and..." I turned to Kim. He was perusing the drinks board. He was another of these people who liked the weird and wonderful.

"An espresso and a Chai tea with soya milk and honey please, no sugar."

I paid while desperately thinking of something to say to her, but nothing worthwhile came to mind. She told us to take a seat and she would bring the drinks over.

I recognised none of the customers as we took a seat next to the counter-side window. Sun was pouring into the café illuminating everything. With the glass front, it seemed like a stage and we were the characters, playing roles for people to see. He recalled his arduous journey from Kingston that morning, we both agreed on the appalling nature of the London public transport system, then the small talk finished.

"Nice place here, never been down this street before. So what's new?" Kim said smiling. I suddenly became very aware of my stomach, like the moment you peak on a roller coaster just before the dive. The only thing missing was the excitement of anticipation. I was unable to control myself. Although words would not exit my body, salt water began to find a way and I scrunched my face up to try and keep it in by sheer force of will. At first Kim didn't register my response, but when I continued to make faces, he realised by the silence.

"Craig, what is it?" he said.

Marie-Louise took this moment to bring the drinks over and I could feel her eyes on me. I could not face her and I saw Kim make some hand gesture, probably reassuring her that everything was all right. He repeated his question. I was unable to speak quietly and decided to just sob to myself until I could. I waved Kim's three-peated question down to ask for more time. When composure started to heal my face, all I could manage with a deadened voice, was 'Kate'.

"Take your time. Are you happy to stay here or do you want to go somewhere with less people?"

Despite the embarrassment of looking a fool in front of Marie-Louise, I felt strangely comfortable. It had become a familiar place in the last week and with the absence of all the other people I had met here, it felt as good as being at home where I would be reminded of the past two years.

"I'm okay here." I took a deep breath and dried my eyes with a tissue from the table. "Basically, we've split up." That was it! I could try and offer interpretations, explanations and justifications, but why bother. That was the whole ball game right there. Kim paused a sufficient amount of time, maybe to avoid bombarding me with questions.

"As in forever or for a while?"

"Forever." I managed on the downhill of breathing out. "Well, pretty much. It looks like forever."

"When did this happen?"

"In the last couple of weeks. She moved out on Saturday. Well, she moved out before, but she moved out her stuff for good on Saturday." I looked down at my coffee and noticed my tears had made dents in the crown. It now looked like a sepia snapshot of the North Pole from above, with huge expanses of dark, murky depths between golden snow. She had taken everything that was hers, except for the odd decorations in the flat that we had bought together. She hadn't even left a note. Since then I hadn't heard from her. In fact, I hadn't heard from her since the last time we sat together in the café.

"Was there a particular reason?"

"Basically, she was quiet for a few days. One day she came home and said she didn't love me, or at least she didn't know if she loved me. I mean, it was messy for a few days. I tried to get her to talk, but she just wanted to act like sleeping in separate rooms was a normal thing to do. Like there was nothing up. It got ridiculous, with me trying to find out what was wrong and playing happy families at the same time. Then she just didn't come back one night, and that was when I realised she had moved out. I think she has someone else already."

"You think she's seeing someone else?" Kim said this with both surprise and remorse which led me to question for the first time, if it might actually be true. It would have been easy just to mention the intriguing parts and make it seem like she had simply taken the first rescue boat on the scene, but I couldn't do that to her.

"Well, I know there is a guy. I know he likes her. At least she has told me he likes her, but she says nothing is happening."

"Do you believe her?"

"Does it matter? She has left, so it's really irrelevant if she is with him or not."

"Possibly", Kim offered a little quieter.

"What do you mean, possibly?" He paused longer to plan his course through the minefield.

"Maybe she just wants some time. If she is with this guy that's one thing, but it is possible she really doesn't want anything from him except an ear to listen to her."

"But if he likes her, it's only a matter of time until something happens."

"Well *that's* not true and you know it. She does have her own mind you know." He waited a sufficient amount of time for me to yield. "Were you having problems for long? Were you talking?"

"I guess talking less and less. You know what it's like. You start to take each other for granted. I wouldn't say things have been bad, but we haven't had a high for a while."

"Is this why you aren't at work?"

"Yeah. I took holiday last week, but I went to the doctor's this morning."

"About this or something else?"

"God, what is this, twenty questions?" I snapped. I realised not only had Kate said this the last time I saw her, but that this was unfair on Kim. However, I had been bottling everything up inside me for so long I just needed to lash out. Kim stayed silent. "Sorry. Well I initially just phoned in sick, but realised that would mean I still needed to go to work tomorrow and I don't think I can face it. So I thought I'd better go to the doctor's to try and get some more time off."

"What did he say?"

"I told him everything. I cried. Felt like a sap. He offered me pills. I said no. He said there was no shame in it. We talked some more and now I have a prescription and three weeks off work."

"How do you feel about that?"

"Did you train to be a psychiatrist?" I attempted an ironic smile to show there was no malice intended. "I don't really want to take them. He asked me a lot about the last few months and my life and to be fair to him, he took his time. He suggested it may be part of a larger thing, and I might have been down for a while." I refused to say depressed. I hate the word.

"Why..." Kim started to smile, as if realising he was about to ask another question. A smile rose from my stomach and it felt good to look through fully open eyes again. We both chuckled.

"I guess I did paint a rather bleak picture of my life to him. I didn't do it intentionally, but the more I spoke, the more I seemed to identify things that I was unhappy with: I have no social life; I hate my job, ripping people off all day; I haven't been out of the country for years; I have the same bloody routine every week; I have less contact with my friends, which I realise is my fault as well; and I guess there was very little I offered him that I felt positive about. He said that some people's bodies just have a certain shortage of something – I forget the name – and there's nothing to be ashamed about by taking a pill to correct this shortage, and if taking one pill a day made me feel better, was there really a big problem in that? It seemed to make a lot of sense to me on the spot, but sitting here now, I still feel like there must be something wrong with me if I can't be happy without taking a pill. I mean other people manage it. I have enough money, a nice apartment, I had a girlfriend and I have great friends and there is nothing really stopping me from doing what I want. Except...I can't really bring myself to want anything. Nothing excites me."

There was a bit of a longer pause while we sought refreshment. Kim sat there patiently as if I was his girlfriend doing my make-up before a big night out. I wiped the tears off the table, drank a little more, wiped away the stains from my face, fixed my hair which felt like it had joined a conspiracy to embarrass me, cleared my voice and then finally looked out the window.

Two years of my life and nothing to show for it. I felt like a tree stump, my essential feature cut down, my roots still entangled in something that was no longer of use to me. I couldn't think of a thing I had done without remembering her, or relating it to her. Even Miles's stag do: she came up to Edinburgh to stay in a hotel so that when the partying ended I would crash back into bed with her. Had it really been two years? Kim broke the silence.

"Do you remember when I broke up with Linsay?"

"Say who?" I snickered. It was a joke we had at the time, can't even remember why it was funny, but it used to wind Kim up. "Yeah, it was a while ago, what particularly."

"If you remember, I broke up with her after about sixteen months. At the time, everyone, including myself, didn't know why. You yourself told me that I was simply no longer in love with her. And you made me realise, I did the decent thing for both of us by ending it. Sure I could have carried on, but as you said, in the long run she would prefer me to finish it sooner rather than later."

I looked down at my coffee knowing what was coming.

"You may not feel it now, but it's much better that she told you. And you too would prefer it in the long run. And you will get over it. I know it doesn't help now, and I know it doesn't feel like it now, but you will get over it. *And* you will meet someone else. OK, she'll get bored of you and go off with someone far better looking and more interesting, but hey, you will have had her for a little while."

This last part he said with a 'you know you want to smile' look, and I couldn't help but give in, if only for a couple of seconds. I engineered a change of subject and asked Kim about his studies and how things were going. He kept his answers concise, but filled me in. He should be starting a placement in Mali later this year if things go to plan and before that he would work for three months at his father's museum in Brighton to placate him. Things with Kim and his girlfriend Marlise were fine. They were going on holiday to South Africa, her homeland, next month after his final oral examination. He had also just written a piece on some tribe I had never heard of, which was being published in some periodical I had also never heard, next month. I had never felt so antithetic to Kim. My life was littered with black holes, a dull job and no decisiveness, and I really envied him and his structure. What I would give to have any of those things lined up for me in the coming weeks.

Customers had exchanged seats, new for old, the typical ebb and flow of a café. Paul had returned. It felt like he deliberately kept his distance, which I interpreted as him being nice. A few more people came in for take-out and I noticed the lunch hour was over. We continued to talk about mutual friends and planned a night out later that week. I wasn't up to much, so we settled on going to a restaurant. He agreed to go to my work place and hand in the doctor's note to my manager. I realised I would have to talk to my manager on the phone, but I really didn't want to deal with him in person. I can't imagine anything more loathsome than crying in front of your boss.

I was quite absorbed until I heard a 'goodbye' and saw Marie-Louise heading for the door, bag in hand. We responded in kind, but I could barely look at her, convinced I still had swollen eyes. Paul was chatting with some guy in a long fawn coat. The guy had untamed hair and from behind, only his large boots could be seen as evidence of other clothes. He looked like a punk with a complete absence of black. He was leaning up against the cake display and his left hand was fiddling with a deck of cards on the counter. Kim broke the silence.

"I guess at some point I have to start getting back. I have to swing by the uni today to give back some books, but I will see you on Wednesday night. I'll meet you here at six, OK?"

"Six it is. Thank you for...well, you know."

"Don't mention it. Give me a bell later. We can have a chat, or hook up on the net and see if any of the gang are around, but I won't say anything to them if you don't want me to."

"Thanks, I appreciate that. I'm going to hang around here a little longer so you go ahead. Speak to you later."

"Take care."

I was suddenly very aware of sitting alone and began to feel more exposed, as if I was camping out and someone had just slashed a gaping hole in the side of my tent. I started to think about my envy for Kim and his life, and the more I thought about it, the more I realised it was not deep. If you had offered me a trip to South Africa, or Mali, or working in a museum in Brighton two months ago I wouldn't have given it a moment's thought before turning it down. Why would I have wanted to do any of those things? With my flat, job, and girlfriend, what would doing any of those things have done to enhance that? When I was in control of things, I rarely wanted for anything. I had little discontent and was happy to live the normal day-to-day life. However, when that was wrenched away from me, I suddenly became desperate. I was open and willing to reach out for anything I could concentrate on. I was no longer in control of deciding what I wanted and I couldn't believe that in the space of a few days my world had turned upside down. 'You don't know what you got till it's gone.' It was a cliché, but a bloody good one.

It was while wallowing in this desperation that I decided to text Kate. It was a simple message: thinking about you. It was ambiguous enough as to not appear slushy, but I felt too hurt to write the truth:

missing you. I stared out the window for a few more minutes before picking up both cups and returning them to the counter.

"Hi Craig. Nice weather today, you got any plans?"

The question he asked drew attention to my absence of things to do. I realised with my doctor's certificate, that absence would now extend for three weeks. I started to feel melancholic, but spoke before it took hold.

"No, nothing special. Just enjoy the sun while it lasts. How was Marie-Louise, good first day?" The other guy was playing with his cards, and playing tennis with his head watching every exchange between Paul and me.

"Seemed very good, nothing fazed her. I even had to leave her alone for a while and it didn't seem to bother her."

"She working every day?"

"Except for a day off in the week."

"I better get off now."

"Have a nice day." The other guy mumbled the same wish. I felt a little uncomfortable not knowing whether to address him, especially since we had not been introduced, but it was too late for me to do that now and sound sincere. I walked out into the sun, smog and emptiness of Camden on a Monday afternoon.

Chapter 7

The next day I was too embarrassed to go the café. I felt I would look as if I had no friends I could meet with, which in London was practically true, but I didn't want others to know that. I spent most of the day anticipating a text or a call from Kate, but nothing came. My desire to talk with her and sort something out was quickly evaporating and turning into frustration.

I arrived at the café on Wednesday morning like the first day after a holiday. As I walked through the door a little after eleven, I saw Marie-Louise, jacket on, moisturising her hands frantically. I thought it a little early for her to be leaving and couldn't imagine why she would do it if she was still serving drinks.

"Off somewhere nice?"

"'Allo Craig, 'ow are you?"

"Good thank you. Do you have the rest of the day off?"

"Oh, no I have some things I have to do now: bureaucracy." She mispronounced the word, but it was sexy nonetheless. Besides, I couldn't ever imagine learning the French word for bureaucracy, let alone spelling it and using it in context.

"A short day then. Nice weather at least."

"Actually, Paul is allowing me to go as I said I would come back later this afternoon to help tidy up. He wanted to show me how to close the shop as well."

"I guess I will see you then. I'm meeting my friend here later. Is it still going well?"

"Yes. Paul is ever so nice. And I met Thomas."

"Thomas?" I instantly regretted letting on I didn't know who Thomas was.

"Yes. From Angola?"

"Oh, Thomas! Sorry, for a minute there I was completely lost." I made a stab in the dark that Thomas was the strikingly tall assistant on Saturday. "I haven't seen him for ages."

"He is lovely. Very quiet, but beautiful speaking voice."

"Aha." I agreed with limitless reluctance.

"So are you coming back for the game this evening?"

One day away and already I felt out of the loop! I surveyed the café for familiar faces. Donna was sitting by the window, and Paul was talking to Matt. I recognised a couple of faces from Saturday, but none with names.

"Umm, haven't decided yet. Have they said what the game is?"

"No. Just a board game. He and Thomas were trying to convince me to stay. I am not sure. Anyway, I had better go now. Have a nice day."

She left and Paul came over to serve me. I felt a little shrunken after her departure.

"Marie-Louise tells me you may be coming tonight?"

"Umm, no I think there was a mix up. I wasn't trying to invite myself."

"No problem, the more the merrier. You can come along if you like."

"It's just that my friend is coming. I mean, I've already arranged to meet him here." I didn't want to commit us to anything, but I was mildly bothered at having this arrangement with Kim. The first non-Kate-related social events I had been invited to for months, and they both come on the same night!

"He's more than welcome as well. We can play with six."

"What game is it? Monopoly or something?"

"It's called Metro."

"Never heard of it."

"Most people haven't. It's just a board game, bit like a puzzle, but it's quick and easy and we just get together to have a bit of fun." I must have seemed unconvinced, because he carried on in sales mode. "We usually meet once a week after closing. Thomas is coming, Marie-Louise might stick around, maybe Matt, Bobby K."

The only other person I could think of with a letter for a last name was Malcolm X and I hardly think Bobby K was in his league. Maybe illiteracy was the reason.

"I'm meeting my friend here anyway, and I'll see what he feels like. He might want a quiet night, he has a lot going on at the moment."

Paul seemed to look away in doubt at this comment. Like a good barman: let the customer have the last word, and make sure they are always comfortable. After all, for the customer this is a home away from home. He was merely here to make it more welcoming, with drinks, a smile and no pressure.

"So, what will it be. Coffee?"

"Yeah, something not quite as strong as the French roast, please. Where did you get the idea for the name of this place?"

"The Kennedys? That would be my aunt. She's the one who put up my stake in the café."

"Oh, she's the silent partner."

"You could say that. She died a couple of years ago."

"Shit, sorry, I thought you said...sorry."

"No worries. When she passed away, she left me some inheritance money. I wanted to put it to good use and I thought to take her name might be a nice gesture as well."

"Sounds more American."

"She married an American. Lived in Wisconsin."

A jolly scream resonated.

"How's Donna today?"

"She's happy enough. That reminds me. I need to put her CD on."

"She has a CD?" I couldn't believe she could make music!

"It's just got some tunes on I know she loves. She used to listen to this stuff when I worked at her home. Sadly, she doesn't have much money for new stuff so I make her CDs to listen to. You should come and say hi, she'll be happy to see you."

I didn't feel comfortable saying hi, and I would be amazed if she reacted in any way that indicated she was happy to see me. He handed me my coffee, came back round to my side and started walking over to Donna and Matt.

"Look Donna, someone wants to say hi." As soon as Paul said this, another two customers walked through the door. Paul turned round, mumbling that he had better serve them, and I was left walking towards the table that was now expecting my arrival.

"Hello Donna. Hey Matt. How are you?" I felt like I was at primary school again, putting on a really patronising voice.

"All right geezer" I was glad he recognised me.

Donna made a large raspberry sound and a high pitched squeal. It was like a satisfied kettle informing the room that the water was ready for tea.

"Oh, I hope I haven't upset her?" I felt self-conscious.

"Nah, she's just chuffed to see you that's all."

"Happy? To see me? But surely she doesn't remember me. I barely remember people I spend an hour selling a TV to, let alone someone who said hi to me a few days ago."

"She don't forget friendly faces." I felt rather warmed by these words and as I turned to look at Donna, who was staring intently at me.

"Hello, again."

She squealed once more, but this time I didn't feel the embarrassment of the first time. I noticed she was slowly unfurling her hand towards me as if revealing a precious stone in her palm. I followed it until her arm was fully extended and her hand open and lying flat. As I started to put my hand out she drew hers back. I acknowledged that she had mastered a classic joke and I had fallen hook line and sinker for it.

"She was offering you her hand to stroke." Matt said, laughing.

"To *stroke*?" I shifted uneasily.

"Yeah, it's a nice gesture. Shows she's comfortable with you."

How could someone be so comfortable with me in such a short period of time? A good old handshake was friendly and can be done with anyone, but stroking! That was for lovers and ill family members.

At this point, the opening riff of 'Marblehead Johnson' came over the stereo and Donna squealed louder and started rocking furiously backwards and forwards in her wheelchair. Despite the brakes being on, the wheelchair was moving from its spot and it looked like if she kept this up she might topple forwards. She slowed her rocking pace, but continued occasionally jerking forwards and backwards, waving her tissue in the air. This was coupled with a series of low drawn-out groans a touch higher than a cow's moo.

"You can forget the hand now, she's in her element."

I felt like I was in a zoo, what with all this talk of stroking, Donna's dancing, and vocal contributions. Paul joined us again and I became very aware of what the other customers might be thinking. I glanced around but no-one seemed to be looking in our direction. Either they genuinely didn't care or they were all fine actors.

"I saw Donna wanted you to stroke her. You really are a flirt, aren't you girl?" This was too much! Paul's comment made me feel like we were first-timers in a singles bar being gently egged on by the rest of the crowd.

"Is that all right? I mean the stroking. I mean not that I want to. I don't mean I don't want to, but I mean, I wasn't asking to." I said.

"She loves it. It's her way of saying, you're OK. Believe me if she didn't want you near her, you would know."

"Why, is she aggressive?"

"Donna's not aggressive, but she can be a bit grumpy sometimes. When she is, you can feel like you don't exist. It's not easy getting you to do something when you're like that, is it? Even eating is practically impossible."

I had picked up that when possible, Matt and Paul talked to her rather than talked about her in the third person. It struck me as a simple point, but a nice one. She might not respond to a question or statement the normal way, but that doesn't mean she doesn't know when she is being spoken to and respond.

"Well, I'm sorry for not taking your hand Donna, I was just a little slow. Next time, I will be a bit quicker." I still didn't feel comfortable using the word stroke.

She stopped and peered at me through one eye with her head cocked at an awkward angle. She was perfectly still and I held my breath. Then, she continued rocking and I saw her gaze wander around for something more interesting to focus on. Matt and Paul laughed.

"I guess that's apology accepted."

Matt got up to go to the toilet and Paul said he would look over her. He turned to me.

"So how are things with your friend, the girl?" I was appreciative he kept the words 'friend' and 'girl' in that order. I tried to think of an answer until I realised this might bring me down, or Paul, or both of us. I went for upbeat instead.

"We haven't really spoken. If I am honest with myself, it's over between us. She's moved out."

I felt like I had no need to hide. Instead of trying to fill the gap I just thought about what this meant: it really did seem over. Yet, I hadn't told my friends, except for Kim. I hadn't told my mum, which would admittedly be difficult seeing as how she loved everything about Kate. The first time I took her back to Bristol with me for the weekend, my mum made such a fuss over her, I felt like she was one half of the relationship. She made cakes, asked her her favourite food and then cooked it – risotto. Risotto! My mum never cooks Italian. She thinks the only difference between balsamic and normal vinegar is that balsamic is stored in balsa wood. She also had a day trip planned. I was never quite sure if it was Kate she loved, or if she just wanted me to find someone who could give her a grandchild.

I had also got accustomed to sleeping alone. I hadn't slept in mine and Kate's bed since she had moved out. It wasn't that I was overcome with emotion when I thought of the bed, but it did feel less comfortable and a touch improper. The couch was mine and more homely, at least for the moment.

"I'm sorry to hear that. Do you miss her?"

"Yes and no. I don't feel down all the time, the feelings come and go. But I do feel a little, what's the word? Incomplete. A little aimless...do I mean aimless? I mean like I am just on auto pilot or something. It's been really hard to focus on stuff, or do anything purposeful." I stared at Donna, still thinking about the question. I spoke without giving my lips permission. "I guess I have just been surviving."

There was a noticeable pause.

"Well, there are people who spend their whole lives doing that. There's nothing wrong with it. Sometimes, you have to not worry about achieving or moving forwards, but instead focus on getting by. And when the time is right, you'll move on again, a bit stronger." I saw Matt come back from the toilet and stop by at a table on the way and chat to a couple of girls who looked stereotypically Swedish.

"I thought I would be devastated. I have had the odd cry at home, but it's not dominated my every waking hour. And there are times when I think we weren't right together; and maybe there are some positives to this."

"Listen, this kind of stuff is never formulaic. You will always have somebody come along and give it the old clichés: 'plenty more fish in the sea' or 'you'll meet someone else'. None of that matters. It's what makes us human. We have to adapt. You built a bond, an emotional attachment and now you have to learn to live without it. Not all emotional attachments are good, some are bad."

"Are you trying to say Kate was a bad emotional attachment?" Dehumanising the situation definitely made it more bearable.

"No, but you have to evolve now. We've been doing it for millions of years. I say just suck it up. You live through this adaptation part. Accept the lows, embrace the highs, but remember your life isn't on hold until you get over this. You are still living this part. So when the motivation comes to do something, no matter how small, grab it.'"

"You mean like playing Metro tonight?"

"Exactly. Like playing Metro tonight." He had a point. I had the motivation so I should go out and do something. I decided I was going to phone Kim and ask if he wanted to play Metro rather than waiting until I saw him.

Chapter 8

Predictably I was there early, only ten minutes, but I swear I don't remember ever being late in my life. Kate used to frustrate the hell out of me with her approach to time, whereby she set all the clocks in the flat differently. The bedroom clock was five minutes fast, so when she finally got out of bed, she didn't feel so pushed. The living room clock was about eight minutes slow, so if she was in the middle of a good film she would not feel as bad about watching it and going to bed late. The bathroom clock was a couple of minutes fast, so when she was in the bathroom, she would feel she was running late and not spend so long there. Her own watch was also set a couple of minutes fast for the practicalities of catching the bus. This one confused me though because if there was ever an organisation that ran independent of time, it was the London public transport system.

By contrast, my need for precision timing means I have my own clock on my side of the bed on exact time, so I always know exactly how much time I have. I have a clock in the bathroom on exact time to counter her clock so I always knew exactly how much time I have. On days when she got up earlier than me, I would wander into the bathroom to see my clock had been turned around so as not to distract her from her make-believe time. I have a personal watch that I wear to work, which I keep on the living room table at night, so I always know exactly how much time I have. And of course my mobile is always up to date...you get the picture. I got my own way with the other things like the CD player and the video. I pointed out that there was no point in bending time for the TV when the TV stations ran on exact time. She pointed out that this was frequently not so, but since they were mine I could do what I wanted.

When I walked into the café Marie-Louise was there with Paul, the man who I assumed to be Thomas, and the man who I had seen with the deck of cards a couple of days previous. No Matt or Kim yet. They were all congregating at the back of the café and for a moment no-one seemed to see me. The man with the cards was the first to notice.

"Hey man, how's tricks?"

"Fine, thanks. And how are you all?" A random applause of 'fine' rang out, only Paul deviated.

"I forgot to introduce you guys. Craig this is Bobby K." Why must that letter always be used! We shook hands exchanging pleasantries. "And this is Thomas." Thomas just nodded his head in recognition, still keeping his 'wonderful speaking voice' under wraps. "I just got a call from Matt, he will be a little late, they had some problems at work. Is Kim still coming?"

As if to directly to answer his question, Kim chose that moment to arrive. It was nice to see him, but felt a little strange in this company. Introductions continued and then we all pulled up seats round a table except the proprietor and Marie-Louise. Paul said he had to show her how to cash up and close the shop. The table now pitted me and Kim on one side, against Thomas and Bobby K on the other. Initially there was a stare off. It felt like the precursor to a poker game more than a board game. I searched my mind for something to say, but all I could think about was how long Marie-Louise was going to be. Bobby K broke the silence.

"What you do Craig?"

Normally I felt quite comfortable talking about my job, but there was something about him that set me on edge. He was without style or sophistication and appeared like he had just been thrown together in haste. Contrary to the look of his clothes, which was of a homeless person, he was not accompanied by any unpleasant smells or skin disorders. His green doc martins seemed to be growing up his legs, masticating his army style trousers. His clothes all looked hard-wearing, like they had grown calluses, and were enclosed in a huge fawn trench coat.

"I'm a salesman." I felt like a corporate whore.

"Of what?"

"Electrical products."

"Cool. What 'bout you man?" He had turned his attention to Kim. I was relieved he seemed happy with my answer, as if I had just passed a test. Or maybe he was just going to compare us to see who was the easiest catch.

"I'm studying." I guess that makes me the easiest catch.

"What d'you study?"

"African Studies."

"Neat!"

Kim continued "What about you two?"

"Thomas works here." At this point, I began to wonder if Thomas was mute. After all, I hadn't actually seen or heard him speak. Marie-Louise had said he had a beautiful speaking voice so he must speak to the women at least. Apart from having to slouch in his chair to reach our eye-level, he was very well built. He sported a smile which despite never leaving his face, seemed to be ever changing and not always appropriate, like he was rolling a die to choose which one to use. His appearance was fastidious and his clothing, immaculately ironed like a golf green. If you looked in the dictionary under Bobby K, it would have said Thomas under antonyms.

"I be in the employment of Her Majesty's Government."

"*You* are in the civil service" I blurted out wishing I had not brandished the 'you' like a spear.

"Yeah man. Go to them every two weeks. They're kind enough to provide me with money while I look for a better option."

Despite only appearing to be in his twenties, his face looked live in, with deep wrinkles that were probably brought about more by wild living than stress, and his light brown hair was spiked up in no particular style except to mock gravity.

I couldn't take my eyes off him and I was sure they were betraying some of the hostility I was feeling. When I finally dragged them away

I found Thomas and Kim laughing. Was it possible that he was such a stereotypical person? He moved on to Kim.

"Wha's African Studies entail, man?" Bobby said.

"Everything: language, religion, anthropology, culture, those kinds of things."

"Any particular countries?"

"I focused on sub-Saharan Africa." Bobby seemed to be awaiting more from Kim. "You really want to know more?"

"Wouldn't ask if I didn't care."

"OK. We looked at language, and very closely at cultural aspects such as religion, literature, art. We also studied the political division of the continent through colonisation and how that affected modern development."

"Always amazed me how big a role a tiny country like Belgium played in such a vast continent."

I couldn't help but check myself. Did I really just hear Bobby K talk about African history? I had little to add to the conversation knowing nothing about it, and it went down an inevitably more serious path about poverty, leading to Thomas's Angolan heritage, at which point I allowed my mind to wander.

It wandered in the direction of Marie-Louise and Paul. He was standing over her while she was counting money, then he showed her how to fill in figures on slips of paper. Everyone seemed content. Several times I saw them lock eyes and occasionally hold them for a little longer than seemed natural.

I realised ashamedly that I was supposed to be spending time with Kim and I was instead pre-occupied with the whereabouts of Marie-Louise. I glanced over to my friend and saw that he seemed to be engrossed in conversation. Kim always could get on with anyone and everyone. He was a wonderful chap and great fun to be with, but he could also be rather difficult. He had a habit of becoming intense from time to time. Every twelve-to-eighteen months he would have a month when he would rarely leave his flat, and give up talking completely. When you live in a flat with him, as I had, this was really not the ideal ingredient for a harmonised household. He claimed that if I tried it, I would appreciate why he did it as its benefit could not be explained, merely experienced. He said the freedom he gained from not speaking was liberating. I failed to see how muteness equals freedom. Try conducting a telephone conversation with a mute! Everyone else seemed to find it endearing – the hairdresser, the corner shop owner, the electricity man. Personally, I just thought he was striving to be different to everyone else by doing something special.

Tonight however, I realised he was happy as long as I was and figured he didn't care if he was talking to me or Bobby. I turned my full attention to Marie-Louise. She was at that moment having Paul peering over her shoulder, supervising her cashing up. Why couldn't I get to peer over her shoulder? I walked over to the scene of the crime.

"So when is the game beginning, Paul?"

"In a minute, I guess. We'll just finish up here. I'm sure she could do it on her own, but this way we get done quicker and can start quicker."

"You can go ahead and play if you want. I don't mind finishing up here while you play." Marie-Louise almost seemed to be excusing herself from the game. This called for an intervention.

"Nonsense, we can wait. And besides, we need one more to make it up to six. It's better with six, isn't it, Paul?" Having never heard of this game before today I hoped it was better with six.

"Er yeah, I guess so," Paul said.

"See! If you don't play, it's worse for us. We'll wait."

"Thank you." She bathed me in a warm smile and I basked.

"That's settled then."

I was rather pleased with myself and the way I had managed to manipulate the situation. Then Matt entered, and the door closed on my smile.

"Hey, just in time, we were about to start without you."

"Sorry, got held up at work, Donna flipped out an' had us running up the walls." I tried to imagine what this situation would look like; a person who cannot walk, or even sit up on her own, 'flipping out'. Did she throw tissues at them? Did she pee all over the chair? Did she refuse to eat? How hard could it be? Whatever she did, why couldn't she have done it for longer? Matt was about to come and spoil a perfect evening.

"Please Paul, you go ahead and play, I can finish up here", Marie-Louise offered.

"Are you sure? I don't mind sitting out and finishing up if you want to play, Lou."

My elation at his offering up his seat to her was eclipsed by the pet name. How dare he call her Lou!

"You love these games, and so does Matt. I can finish up here. I need the practice. If I have questions I will ask."

"I can help her", I said rather desperately. "That way she is finished quicker and we can all play."

"But didn't you say it was better with six, Craig?" said Marie-Louise.

"Well *ideally*...but we can't all have ideals, can we?"

"Come on, Craig", I heard Paul say with indistinguishable politeness and force. I felt like a defeated schoolchild being ordered by mum to stop misbehaving. What was there left to do, except ignore mum?

"But I wanted to ask Marie-Louise about something I thought she could help me with." Please don't ask what, please don't ask what.

"About what?" I scrambled around inside my brain looking for something to link with Marie-Louise I could ask her about.

"I was interested in going on holiday to France and I wondered if you could recommend somewhere." The ground was slowly parting before me and starting to feast upon my lies. I heard Paul call my name again, but I was on a role now.

"Well..." she started. I was winning her over, but Paul intervened.

"Look, sorry Craig, but this is Marie-Louise's first time doing this, and I would prefer it if she didn't have any distractions, just to make sure it's all spot on. You come and play and then you can chat when we've all finished."

"But I'm going out with Kim later?" Now I was even pleading like a child.

"Well, ask her tomorrow. You're not going on holiday this week, are you?"

Paul was getting the better of me. I was just about to answer affirmative, until I realised this would mean avoiding the café for a few days and that I definitely didn't want. I needed to save face.

"That's a great idea." *Great idea?* "I can speak to you tomorrow. We can chat for longer then."

"Oh, sorry Craig, but I am not working tomorrow. How about Friday. Is that OK?"

"Perfect". The absolute adjectives were flowing now.

As I trudged back to the table, Paul showed me the first negative facial expression I had seen since I had met him – it was disappointment. All I could think of though, was the next hour or however long it took to play this game. I did not want to play with a group of people, of which half I had no interest in spending time with, when the person I really wanted to spend time with was a few feet away, unreachable.

Begrudgingly, I must admit the game was actually quite enjoyable. I couldn't fully concentrate, but it didn't require total immersion. The board was a square and had empty spaces to place tiles. On each tile there were several train routes and every tile linked to the routes of every other tile. Each tile stemmed from train stations which players had scattered around the edge of the board. You placed your tiles trying to extend your own train routes and block off other people's. The longer your routes, the better. Matt won the game and Thomas fared worst. This had nothing to do with the poor public transport system in Angola, yet this didn't stop Bobby K bringing it up and discussing Africa some more with Kim. Thomas also spoke, although I think it was mostly swearing in some unknown dialect when someone blocked him off.

All the time, Marie-Louise was concentrating on her work, and every time I managed a glance in her direction, I failed to catch her eye. As the game wore on, my glances became less and less frequent. Finally, twenty minutes before what was to be the end of the game, although I did not know this at the time, Marie-Louise announced she had finished. She said she had had a long day and wanted to go home and get an early night. Nailed to the floor by the game, no protests I could have made would have bore fruit, and rather dejectedly, I accepted that I would not get to spend any time with her that night.

After she left, Paul pulled out a card game and the newly assembled group of disparate beings started to relax. The rest of the evening was very nice and Kim was happy to stay and play. The card game was about planting beans in fields and then selling them for gold, which really was better than it sounds, causing much frustration and hair pulling. I found out that Bobby's 'K' stood for Kindle, but since he had experienced much luck in previous years, his friends had often called him Kismet, or Karma, and faced with this choice, they merely shortened his surname to K. When I asked what luck he had experienced he informed us. He had survived: a house fire despite being asleep; a car crash when knocked off his bike by a lorry; and falling out of a boat in the North Sea whilst fishing. All this suggested to me that he was a rather unlucky person, and gave me the eerie feeling that he was not safe to be around. In between games, he took to fiddling with his deck of playing cards.

"What's in there?" I asked.

"Lucky joker."

"Sorry?"

"My lucky joker. It's a lucky token. Always had it with me through thick and thin."

"So why not just carry the joker?" I realised I was starting to sound a little aggressive. "I mean, I agree if it brings you luck, it's a good idea to keep it near you, but surely it's a drag to carry a whole deck around?"

"Joker gets lonely."

I paused for the laughs around me so I could join in, and when they didn't come, I was stuck between releasing my laugh or bottling it up. It came out, sounding like a discreet cough in a library. As I looked around, no-one was paying attention to this conversation. It was as if they had either heard it before, or as though we were talking about some long lost aunt. Bobby's face betrayed no emotion either and I had the unnerving feeling he was serious.

Paul enlisted liquid reinforcements, caffeine flowed, walls came down, and bonds were made. I was happy to note on the way home later that night, that after she had left, Marie-Louise had become only a pin prick in my mind.

Chapter 9

The first thing I thought about when I woke up was Marie-Louise. I was quickly arrested by my guilt and started to think about Kate. I wondered what she was doing now, guessing she was working. I couldn't get my head around what had happened. Three weeks before I was living in mundane bliss with a dull, but solid future, and now I felt like I was trying to tread water in quicksand. I was losing interest in my job – the most stable thing I had left. Instead, I was being drawn in the direction of Marie-Louise and the café. Surely I couldn't really feel something for her? After all, a week ago, I would have said without hesitation I was in love with Kate, even if not to her face. I seemed to be avoiding any semblance of structure. Furthermore, I subscribed to the time-honoured consensus that a problem is only a problem if you think it is. The less I thought about Kate, I kidded myself, the less of a problem I had. I had been behaving like a spoilt kid: wanting what I couldn't have, and unwilling to compromise.

What would I do if Kate asked me back today? Agreed, it looked unlikely, but it was a valid question. I realised one of the reasons I had avoided committing myself was because I had too much wounded pride. I hypothesised upon reasons why I might get back with her: she was very caring; she would never deliberately hurt me; she was comforting; I felt whole when with her, like a cup with its saucer; I certainly felt more temporary now and didn't enjoy that. When I thought about the situation, a cloud of mist appeared to descend upon my mind. Instead of stumbling around arms outstretched and bumping into things, it was easier to just lie down and wait for the mist to clear. I went back to sleep.

The first thing I thought about when I woke up the next time was Kate. But, should I just dismiss any feelings I might have for Marie-Louise? That day, Thursday, she wasn't working and so I decided to take a break from the café. Then I began to think this might be too obvious to Paul. Who was I kidding? He knew exactly how I felt about her. And he knew about Kate and I would rather Marie-Louise did not know about that part of my life at the moment. I decided to smooth things over with Paul. So like the true regular I aspired to be, I went traipsing off to The Kennedys once again.

A thing about regulars is that they avoid other strange communities by spending their time in one safe place, and consequently form their own community. Regulars in a coffee shop, as opposed to say an establishment that serves alcohol, don't really mingle. Nevertheless, they accept and respect the fellow regulars there. It doesn't take long for these people to start recognising one another and exude warmth with stretched smiles of recognition. A café, often has regulars of all ages and backgrounds; pubs tend to get grouped into particular demographics more easily than cafés.

The Kennedys was no different and had its own brand of the weird and wonderful to which I had now become affiliated. One of the first I noticed was Jam Man. Whenever possible, he sat in the corner of the café and got attention by ignoring the world. That Thursday, I realised I had seen him there before, but never really processed him. Like all good regulars, he had that quality of blending in as if part of the furniture, yet was in possession of something unique that set him apart.

Jam Man always ordered two muffins, usually apple muffins. He also always had a pot of jam and a spoon with him. Seeing as Paul didn't sell jam I deduced that it must be his own. He looked a bit like an eighty-year old Hunter S. Thompson. He usually wore a beige knitted flat cap, chequered trousers, an orange jumper, and a brown flying bomber jacket with a military insignia on it. The jacket had a fur collar, and when open, revealed a large gold cross on a gold chain hanging between the zipper, that cried out for attention. His glasses were thick-rimmed and he sported a wild grey moustache, growing with the sole purpose of finding a way off his face. None of this was particularly distracting. It would be were it not for his quirky eating ritual. First, he would break off a piece of muffin and hold it in his left hand, lift the lid off the open jar of jam, spoon a generous helping onto the piece of muffin, replace the lid, and then make the journey to his mouth, meeting it halfway by moving his face towards the trembling jelly.

What grabbed everyone's attention, was that when he ate, he sounded like a horse clopping on puddles of water. The sound got louder the more you looked at him. It was not possible to avoid looking in his direction for more than thirty seconds. Every time you started to think you could ignore his presence, the sound cajoled your ears into persuading your eyes to pay attention and look at him. It was mid-afternoon and I saw him as the café window came into view, the untouched second muffin lay there fearfully.

Paul was behind the counter and as soon as I entered he gave me a welcoming grin. It made me feel better after having spent the morning doubting whether he would want me here again so soon. I ordered my usual.

"I picked up a little something for you, just to say sorry about last night. I was being a bit of a..." He realised I was a man overboard and waiting for a life belt, which he obligingly threw me.

"Don't worry about it. I know things have been tough, I just really wanted Marie-Louise to concentrate on her work. It was her first time cashing up."

I pushed my package across the counter towards him.

"Go on then, open it."

"Looks interesting." He picked it up and shook it and heard a lonely rattle of copper on ceramic. "Curious!" When he unwrapped it he was face to face with a pale green money pig, with a one penny coin inside to get the ball rolling.

"I figured you have no donation box, and you always seem to listen to people. Well, me at least. This might be a chance to let people say thanks. I've never been in a café without one."

"I guess when I see them in other cafés, I always feel obliged to put money in and feel bad if I don't. I don't want people to feel that way here."

"Well, some people just like to show thanks. And I can't stand to collect five pence coins, so it's one way to get rid of them."

"Thank you, Craig. We are having another games night tonight if you like, you're more than welcome."

"Thanks, but I think I need to have a night in and sort some things out."

"Sounds serious?"

Marie-Louise walked in.

"'Allo."

"What are you doing here?" I blurted out like an incompetent interrogator. "It's your day off!"

"I 'ave some things to do in Camden. Could I have a latte please, Paul?"

"I'm on it."

"What are you doing today, Craig?"

I wasn't sure if this was polite conversation or if she was asking for a date.

"Oh, just hangin' out with Paul." Why oh why, did I drop the 'g' off hanging? Now I was really starting to sound like an aimless bum. I needed goals. "Um, I also have to return some books to the library...and some other things." Suddenly my life seemed so busy. If I ever feel like I have nothing to do, I can just talk to Marie-Louise for two minutes and suddenly have a full day.

"But you have no bag." She was looking around where I was standing, pulling a face like she was trying to remember the first fifteen digits of Pi. I was flattered she noticed what I did and didn't have, but couldn't help wondering why she was so concerned about my lack of a bag.

"That's right, no bag." I even smiled at Paul to show my confusion at her line of questioning.

"What about your library books?" I held the smile for a few seconds more as if she had not spoken. Suddenly, I realised she was a third of an audience awaiting a response, along with Paul and Jam Man. I feigned ignorance to the question.

"What?"

"I just wondered where your library books are? I see no books."

I cursed her directness.

"Well no, of course not. I realised I left them here, but then Paul said I hadn't so they must still be at home. Oh well, at least that's one less thing to do."

"Oh, okay."

Seemed easy. Mental note, when faced with a tough question, just act like a bumbling idiot.

"Did you say yesterday you wanted to ask me some questions about France. I have a few minutes before I am meeting my friend."

Once again, I was presented with a less than ideal way of spending a few minutes with her. We would have to spend the whole time talking about my imaginary trip to France and then she would leave. This was no good.

"Actually, I am a bit pushed for time at the moment. Can we do it some other time? When we both have a free window."

"Sure. I am here tomorrow and you seem to be here most days."

Was the 'you seem to be here most days' meant as a genuine observation or a sad indictment? I cursed the time I had spent in this café. I needed to get a new life. One which I could fit her into instead of one I fit around her.

"Anyway, I gotta run now, places to go, people to see."

"What about your coffee?" she asked.

"Oh yeah." I laughed unconvincingly loudly. "Can I get that to go, Paul?" Paul dispensed the coffee into a take-away cup – I normally abhor them. These plastic/cardboard cups were not meant to drink coffee from: if I was that desperate, I would make the time and be late for an appointment. "Ciao", I managed with enthusiasm, and left the café with the wrong kind of bitter taste in my mouth.

I started scouting for a bin to place my coffee in, and as I rounded the corner I saw a homeless man sitting on a sleeping bag. Realising how callous it would be to throw it away in his sight, I walked over to him and handed him the coffee. He appeared to double take when he looked at it.

"Is there sugar in it?"

"Sugar! I suppose you also want milk?"

"You got some?" He looked as if my generosity had put him in a tough situation, which I guess if he only liked coffee when it was with sugar and milk, he was. He seemed terribly young to be out on the street and although his clothes looked hygienic, his face was quite grubby and he appeared unwilling to make eye contact.

"Not on me, sorry."

He put the coffee down on the pavement and shifted himself. I suddenly had the fear he might not drink it.

"No worries", he said, "thanks anyway."

If he was not going to drink it, my pitiful gesture – offering up a drink I wasn't going to drink anyway – would seem somewhat worthless.

"Would you like me to get you some?" I was sure he would say no, but at least my conscience would be clear.

"Yeah, cheers."

I blinked at him, a little in disbelief, until I reminded myself, I had actually asked him a valid question and received a valid response. I surveyed the sky and saw a darkening horizon.

"OK hold on. You want anything else?"

"Sugar and milk's fine."

I considered going to the Bean Cup to get some, but seeing as that would involve walking in the opposite direction to my arrival, I thought he might think I was doing a runner. I breathed, squirmed and headed back to The Kennedys.

As I walked in, Paul was leaning over the counter, very relaxed, his face in close proximity to Marie-Louise's. Once again, a shot of jealousy nicked my heart and I felt like I had turned up on his own doorstep unannounced. Paul saw me first.

"Craig, to what do we owe this honour again so soon?"

"I forgot sugar."

"Hang on, aren't you the one who thinks sugar kills the taste of coffee?"

"Well, I guess I just need some extra energy." I wasn't sure how much the guy wanted, so I grabbed a few bags. Then I saw the mini takeaway milk cartons and took a couple of them as well.

"Milk as well, now I've seen it all."

"A man can change, can't he?" I said, sharper than intended.

"Hey, it's your coffee. As long as you still like it enough to come back, I am happy."

"Cheers, have a nice day." Just as I reached the door and felt like I had got away lightly, Paul raised his voice again.

"Just one more thing, Craig. Where did you put your coffee?"

I realised I had come back to get milk and sugar for a coffee I no longer had. I paused and it was long enough to expose any potential lie I might tell before I spoke. I was growing weary of putting myself in these situations.

"Actually, I gave it to some homeless guy. The milk and sugar are for him." With that I left. I actually felt quite happy about it, although as I saw Paul lean back over the counter and probably share a joke about my incompetence. It was then I worried that Paul might actually be making a move on her. There was little I could do about it even if I wanted to. I could barely spend five minutes with her and he got to spend most days in her company.

I handed the homeless guy his milk first. I quickly felt that I had done nothing for this guy compared to what was possible. He had helped me out by taking a bad coffee off my hands, but when the rain started in an hour, I would be cooped up warm in my flat and he would still be sitting here. I slipped a five pound note into the bundle of sugars to ease my embarrassment at having a more comfortable life than him. As I trudged towards the bus stop, I wondered what his coffee tasted like. I hadn't tasted coffee with milk and sugar in years.

Chapter 10

I knew Marie-Louise was shutting up shop again the next day. Also, earlier in the week Paul had told me he had an appointment with a company about supplying sandwiches daily on Friday afternoon. I planned my trip around the possibility of some time with Marie-Louise and no-one looking over our shoulder. I arrived at the café around five. I managed to waste the day in my flat, most of it cleaning, which helped to occupy my mind and felt like I was doing something worthwhile.

The only reason men clean, is women – either to impress them or placate them. If you live with a woman then it is the latter, and if you want to live with a woman it is the former. It's a kind of (pre-)relationship ritual: without women, men don't clean. Men don't want to expend the energy, and don't have the inclination to even if they did. It's another contributing factor to there being very few male cleaners: we simply can't see the difference between clean and dirty.

Time and time again, Kate and I would spend a Sunday morning cleaning the flat and afterwards she would say; 'See how much cleaner it is. Aren't you happier now?' Of course, I felt unhappier having wasted two hours of my life doing repeated circles with a grubby damp cloth in my hands while bent on all fours. And of course I could not see that it was cleaner. Granted, I could see the dirt on my cloth, but as I could see no difference in the object I was rubbing, it inhibited any potential enthusiasm. Despite this, my answer was always an animated 'yes, much better'. For those who think of me as spineless, and who respond to a female's cleaning suggestions with a simple no, I would argue that this made Kate extremely happy, more from my enthusiasm than any rubbing-related outcome. Those who said no have pissed their woman off, and she will be forever burdened with the thought that they will never clean the house. She will be filled with disappointment as to the kind of slob she has hooked up with. This is where they could point out that I am without a girlfriend and therefore my argument is down the pan. To this, I have no answer except, good point. I curse all those wasted cleaning hours!

As I walked through the door, the April shower chose this moment to cease and the sun made its first appearance of the week. The floor of the café was speckled with the shadows of rain droplets looking like some urban pasture. I noticed some familiar faces in the café. Donna was there, as was Jam Man, and Cushion Man.

Cushion Man was in his fifties, and earned the moniker because he always brought his own cushion. It felt to me as if some people were desperate to stand out. He wore a long, ill-fitting black faded jacket with scuffed black boots. His hair was greasy and unkempt, and he had a nervous twitch that he couldn't control for more than three seconds. Despite the rest of his appearance, every time I saw him he had a pair of immaculate dark blue denim jeans. I surmised that the cushion was to protect the jeans, he seemed to have little else worth protecting. Amongst all these freaks was Marie-Louise, staring at a Sudoku puzzle and moisturising her hands.

I greeted Donna as I passed her table. She was with a carer I had not seen before. Three cups lay on the table, one nearly empty. Her carer smiled in a 'who the hell are you but thanks for saying hi' kind of way. I said hello to her as well and waited for a question that never came. I tried to display my trustworthiness.

"Hi Marie-Louise. How are you?" I offered this a little louder than necessary. Jam Man stirred and looked up from his second muffin.

"Great, thank you. How are you?"

"Can't complain. Well I could, but nobody's listening." It came out like a comic trying to win back his audience with stop gap measures. It didn't bode well for the time ahead. She started making me a coffee.

"Nice weather now."

"It's about time. The best thing about spring is these cool days, with relentless sun and wide blue skies."

"There's a bit of a poet in you!"

She blushed. "No. I think I read those lines somewhere. But really, don't you love days like this?"

"I guess I prefer it to the damp and the rain." I was not cut out for discussions about the weather. After stating the obvious, where do you go from there? It's a precursor to another topic, and I always think why don't we just get down to the other topic?

"What's the weather like in Amboise?"

"You remembered, very good! It's a little warmer I guess, but not much different. Less rain though."

"Tell me about it."

"Amboise?"

"Yeah."

"Let me think. It's a small market town. The Loire River runs through it. We have a castle called Château d'Amboise. Leonardo da Vinci is buried there."

"*The* da Vinci?" Sarcastic native speaking friends of mine would have leapt on this with a comment such as; 'no another Leonardo da Vinci who was a butcher, or baker, or candlestick maker'. I was still smiling at my foolish comment when I realised Marie-Louise had continued speaking without contemplating sarcasm. I cursed myself for having missed what she had said.

"...but he spent the last three years of his life there and is now buried in the Château."

"Do you miss it?"

"I think a part of me is staying there." She paused. She looked as if she had something to add, then changed direction. "What about you, where are you from?"

"Bristol. You know it? It's about a hundred miles west of London."

"What is special about Bristol?"

I exhaled in deep thought. I was ashamed to realise I didn't really know much about it, and said so. I was clearly surprised at the response myself, as though I was being asked what number comes after ten, and realising I had never used it before.

"I never really paid that much attention in school. I know it was bombed a lot during the war. Bristol, not my school. So we have a lot of ugly high-rise buildings." She didn't laugh at my joke, which made me feel a little embarrassed. "It's not the prettiest of cities. We have a big harbour, but really I don't...." I tailed off to think. "The countryside around it though is lovely. Oh yes, and the Clifton Suspension bridge! I've never really thought about it before, but yeah, the Clifton Suspension Bridge is famous."

My sudden enthusiasm seemed to amuse her and at the point of making this minor breakthrough, another customer came through the door. I stepped back to give her some space to take the order and could hear Donna rocking back and forth behind me. The friction of her jacket against the chair was steady and sounded like someone sanding wood. Without music, I could only think she was cheering me on at finally having started a normal conversation with Marie-Louise. It made me feel like Donna was rooting for me. Matt came in and joined her. He drained one of the cups on the table. The other carer bid farewell to both him and Donna, and left.

I took my coffee and found myself reaching for the sugar container. I paused to think if I really wanted any. It seemed stupid to be dwelling over a decision of such minuscule import. I poured a little on my spoon and stirred it in.

The man who came in, seemed to take an age to choose his drink. He leaned back, stared up at the drinks menu and squinted his eyes in a way that was very unbecoming. I was amazed how long he kept this leaning pose and I started to imagine him slowly tipping back. I stepped nearer to him only to realise he was perfectly in control of his balance and that I somehow had to disguise my foolish rescue attempt. I changed direction mid-step and turned it into the first step on the way to the toilet.

It was the first time I had approached the doors at the back. On one of them there were two hand drawn pictures, of a man and woman in Victorian clothing: the woman complete with a crinoline supported skirt, bonnet and umbrella; and the man with a walking stick, top hat and and long town coat. The other two doors sported tastefully scripted signs stating: 'We would appreciate it, if you would refrain from entering these rooms.'

When I returned, it was as if the town had heard that Craig was making progress and decided to come and pull up a chair and watch. Every table was full now, although Cushion Man had moved on, and Jam Man had just finished his second muffin. Matt was sitting comfortably with Donna and offered me a nod of recognition. I sauntered over to the counter and was grateful there was nowhere to sit and no queue.

"So tell me about the Clifton Suspension Bridge."

"It was designed by Isambard Kingdom Brunel and goes over the River Avon. When it was built, it was the longest bridge in the world. It's just a famous landmark in Bristol. You see it on all the postcards. He designed all kinds of firsts, the Great Western Railway, steamships and loads of bridges. In fact, I think there is one over the Thames River which was designed by him." I was on role now.

"Which bridge over the Thames?"

"It think it's the one next to the London eye with the trains over it."

"But that looks really new."

I realised she was right.

"I guess that's the new one. But the original might have been by him."

"You seem to know a lot about him."

"I guess it's natural, seeing as he is such a famous man in British history and it's such a famous local landmark."

"Is Bristol worth a visit?"

"The area around it is. The surrounding counties are lovely, but Bristol itself is like most big cities."

"You don't like big cities, no?"

"Not my favourite. But I guess they are not that bad."

"Didn't you have some questions about France for me?"

"Ah, yes." I sounded grateful, but I still wasn't sure what I was going to say. "Basically my friend and me, are looking to go camping later this year, and wondered if you could recommend some places we should check out."

She seemed elated with my fictional idea.

"My cousin is running a campsite in a really beautiful forest south of Blois. It depends if you were looking to move around or not. It's a great spot to set up camping and explore the Loire Valley with lots of beautiful palaces. I will look into it some more for you, I have a friend who has done a lot of camping around France, she would be better to ask. I am not a big lover of camping." Her dislike for my supposed hobby made me feel a little foolish. I wanted to find out our shared interests.

I always liked camping though, and it was something I wish I did more often. When I was younger, my friends and I always used to go camping in Avon, Somerset or the Cotswolds in the holidays. We would head off discovering our independence and just how close we were attached to modern life when we were without mother's cooking, TV, or games consoles. It was something I needed to look into doing again. Kim used to enjoy it and if he was considering relocating to Africa, he might not be averse to forgoing a few comforts in a tent in Kent or Essex. There was something else I felt I needed to see again: the sea. It was part of my upbringing, like an older brother: a little frightening, but ultimately reassuring and comforting.

"I find it nice to hop into your car, drive off somewhere and sleep in the great outdoors. It's quite liberating." I added this as an afterthought, not convinced myself.

"Do you have a car?"

"No, I sold it when I came to London. It seemed unnecessary, but I do miss it. I don't need it in London granted, but it is nice to have one to get away in."

"I don't like cars. They are such disruptive things."

"Disruptive?"

"And loud, and dangerous *and* dirty."

"Sounds like you had a traumatic experience."

"Seriously, they are, don't you think?" I hesitated as it was not a subject I had thought much about before. I had always just reaped the benefits of the car. I didn't want to find another thing we disagreed on.

"I guess so."

"But England is a perfect example. You have a country with too many cars and not enough space and it makes it so polluted. They are ubiquitous. The last thing you need is more cars."

"Fair enough, I can't argue with the pollution, but still?"

"Still what?" Her response seemed a little melodramatic. I started to sweat and feel like I was on Mastermind and the café was the audience waiting for me to answer. Maybe there is something to the French stereotype of being very passionate. As much as I wanted the passion directed towards me, I didn't want it thrown at me.

"I just don't see why a car is automatically ugly. I think they are wonderful, practical creations." The smile on my face was meant to warm the conversation, but it seemed to remain somewhat cool.

"I am not talking about practicalities."

I paused, avoided making a point, and decided instead to try and understand her argument more.

"You say a car is ugly. What for you is beautiful? What things do you look at as representative of beauty in London?"

"Architecture. You have some wonderful historical buildings in London; St Paul's Cathedral, the Houses of Parliament, the Tower of London."

"But weren't they born out of practicalities? OK, they are great looking and they didn't have to be made to look like that, but essentially they were built to house a purpose, be it the government, the church or protection. Yes, they are old, but then the practical purpose of them was never as hard wearing as the purpose of a car."

"But cars are just lumps of metal!"

"What's so bad about that?"

This seemed to anger her a little. I desperately wanted to get back to talking calmly and quietly and her enjoying my company. Instead, I could see no way out of this. I was drawing on my sales experience to try and pacify the customer and move her on to the end of the transaction, but it was more difficult due to my grovelling.

Paul burst through the door and I had never been happier to see him. He looked at me, in a mock quizzical fashion.

"Don't I know you from some place? You look familiar."

The tension seemed lifted, but I didn't want to risk further clashes and took the diversion that Paul offered.

"Yeah, someone recommended a good café around here and I was just asking this young lady if she knew where it was."

"Beats me. We're all charlatans and crooks around here."

"Oh well, Burger King it is then."

We all laughed in unison, yet mine was garnished in relief.

"Craig is thinking of going camping in France" said Marie-Louise.

"Is that so?"

"Thinking about it. I've always liked camping and wouldn't mind checking out another country. As I have my very own walking guide book here, I thought it best to consult her first."

"Oh, so I am just a guide book now!" Her facial features were all pointing upwards as if gravity had been reversed and she slammed the counter in fake anger at the suggestion.

"You are not thinking of kidnapping my new worker here are you?" As Paul said this, he placed his arm around her and pulled her slightly towards him in psuedo-protection. She seemed amused by his question and looked animated in his arm.

As we continued the small talk, Matt came over and asked us to keep an eye on Donna while he went to the toilet. Paul told him yes, but something made me want to go over and sit with her instead of watching her from afar. I remember how it felt to sit alone in a café with few options, and whereby I had no idea if she was feeling this, I imagined it could be possible.

As I sat down next to her she was completely still. I took a sip of my coffee, but didn't speak. Instead, I just placed my elbows on the table and stared at Donna waiting for her to break the silence. I heard Paul offer some guidance to Marie-Louise about closing. Donna moved her head round slowly like a crane lining itself up. She stared at me, possibly asking why Marie-Louise was drawing my attention from across the room while she sat next to me ready for conversation. I took another sip and broke our silence.

"Do you think I should ask her out Donna?"

She looked straight back at me without flinching, as if she was frozen.

"Is that a no, or an I don't care?" I paused but still she didn't move. I looked down and saw she still had some coffee left in her cup.

"Do you want some coffee, is that what you want?" I put my hands round the cup as if to solidify the offer and with this she turned her head away while making a low shriek like a creaky door hinge upon closing. Then she started waving her tissue around. I picked up the cup and held it out for her, offering her the handle as I had seen Matt do before. Donna reached for it with her good hand after dropping the tissue and drew it slowly to her lips. She slurped it up and I felt a warm sense of satisfaction as she drank the remainder. I sat there for a moment sharing her world. She had left her hand on the table after she had placed the empty cup back on it. I reached out and considered stroking it. It still felt wrong, although I couldn't for the life of me explain why. My hand was next to hers and I stretched one finger out and started a circle motion on the back of her hand. She kept her hand there and turned her head round to meet my gaze. I suddenly felt exposed and wondered if anyone else in the café was watching us. As I looked round, everyone else seemed immersed in their own world. I continued circling for about a minute. I drew my finger back when I saw Matt coming back from the toilet.

"Finally finished your coffee, sweety? I guess you were just havin' me on, wantin' to flirt with the men."

I felt a little embarrassed at the suggestion, but understood it more now. Donna was being treated like a normal girl her age and included, instead of assisted.

"Come on young lady, best be gettin' you home for grub."

Paul and Marie-Louise were deep in discussion. It felt good to have had a bit more of a conversation with her and I told myself she was not angry at me. After all, it was not her native language and naturally she might sound a little more direct. I didn't want to distract Marie-Louise from her work again, or put Paul in the same position I had on Wednesday. I drank my coffee and noticed a couple of sugar grains in the bottom of my cup. It had tasted no different to me.

"Mind if I walk with you guys, Matt? Just until you get home. I have a little time to kill."

"No probs."

I held the door open for Donna and Matt as we left. It felt nice to hold the door open for a lady again.

Chapter 11

My weekend was an entirely indoor affair. I spent it wrestling with my lack of motivation to go back to work. I spent it wrestling with, although finding it very difficult to pin down, my feelings for Kate. I spent it wrestling with whether I should ask Marie-Louise out. I had little desire to go to the café in such an unsure state. I had little desire to leave the flat. I had little desire.

Feeling tired through depression rather than activity or lack of sleep, on Monday I arrived at the café early morning. I had another appointment with the doctor in the afternoon and didn't want to go to The Kennedys too close to that in case there was a situation I wanted to prolong. It was ten o'clock and Marie-Louise was there, chatting with a seated, anxious looking Paul. The café was empty.

"Craig, just the man!"

"Nice to see you too. Although, the suspicious side of me wants to ask exactly what I am the man for."

"Go on then."

"How about you just go ahead, and I watch you grovel." Every time Marie-Louise smiled at something I said, it filled me like a balloon and I felt ready to burst with excitement. It was also nice to have someone actually need me for something.

"I have a bit of a problem. Thomas was supposed to be working this morning with Lou, only he's sick. He caught some virus over the weekend. The thing is, we have our delivery coming any minute now, and I have had twinges in my back all weekend. It's not too bad when I sit down, a little painful standing, but I don't really want to risk lifting anything. Sorry to ask, but otherwise Marie-Louise will have to do it. Any chance you could spare an hour."

"And I said it was no problem for me to lift a few boxes." She said turning to me as if to form a side with which to counter Paul's argument. "I am not exactly a helpless female."

There was no way I was going to let Marie-Louise do the order. And Paul had been a genuinely good bloke to me since I met him and the least I could do was help.

"What's in it for me?" I added a smile to let him know I wasn't serious.

"Buy you lunch?"

"You're on."

Marie-Louise did not seem too bothered as it gave her a chance to hover around Paul, making him rest.

When Aaron arrived, the delivery driver, the first thing Paul did was to sit him down at a table with a newspaper and cappuccino and tell him to relax. This seemed odd practice to me. I thought my help would be needed in addition to, not instead of the delivery driver, but it appeared that The Kennedys was Aaron's rest stop. I nonchalantly followed Paul out to the van and he told me what to get in first and only after I insisted, did he go back inside. There was a surprising amount of goods to bring in. I didn't know how often he got deliveries, but there were different teas, milks, hot chocolates, and some food stuffs, although he said he got his coffee from another supplier. That would account for all the different types of roasts he offered alongside the espresso based drinks. Most people asked for espressos, but he himself never drunk them, wanting a more 'authentic taste'. Although he didn't go in for the flavoured syrups, he did go in for different dietary requirements: lactose free, yeast free, sugar free, gluten free. It seemed Paul could provide an absence of anything in his food and drink.

"Where did you learn about all these different special diet foods?" I enquired relinquishing the first box.

"Just picked it up over the years. I had my own fads where I ate different diets. I went yeast free for a while when some dietary specialist told me I had candida."

"Candida?"

"Basically it's yeast intolerance, but I don't really think I had it. At least not as bad as some people I know."

"What happened?"

"I went to her because she was recommended by a friend of mine who had candida. She is allergic to all kinds of things: mushrooms, excess sugar, dairy products, various fruits. I think pretty soon she will become allergic to her husband! She is a nightmare to cook for. Anyway, she had to go on a really strict diet and she knew everything about allergies."

I nodded and went to collect another box. It had a fair-trade stamp on it, and was surprisingly heavy for tea. Paul opened the door for me and picked up the conversation again.

"I've always had problems with nuts and it pisses me off. Sometimes I can eat peanuts and other times not, same with hazelnuts. And some nuts are real no-goers like pistachio. Anyway, I used to get through a kilo of cashews a week, which were about the only nuts I could have which never caused a problem."

I noticed that despite having a thin frame, his belt was embedded in his mid-section and his belly was trying to bail out.

"But then one day I started to have reactions to them. My ex-wife said enough's enough. She was tired of never knowing if I would make it through a meal reaction-free, and insisted I went to see a specialist."

I had never even entertained the thought that Paul was married, let alone divorced.

"What kind of reaction do you get?" I have never had an allergic reaction in my life, unless you could count my becoming short of breath and dizzy after walking in on my parents having sex when I was fifteen, but I get the feeling everyone is allergic to that.

"I get severe headaches, centred around my eyes. Not exactly migraines but very sharp. Oh and I can't breathe." He added this as an afterthought. Surely, this would be first and the headaches would be an afterthought! It would be like answering the question did you have a good weekend with 'yes I went for a lovely long walk in Regent's Park...oh and I won the lottery jackpot!'

"You can't breathe!"

"Well, it's extremely difficult. I sometimes start hyper-ventilating and wheezing and have to lie down and sweat it out."

I was disturbed and grateful I was able to eat what I pleased. Granted, I have the odd thing I hate. I have always found cucumbers less appealing than eating vomit, especially since whenever I had eaten them in the past, this was the usual consequence.

I remember at university we had a blindfold drinking game. After innumerable beers and shots there were about a dozen of us piled into our student kitchen. It started off with us standing round the table and spinning a knife. Whoever had the blade pointing to them was forced to don a blindfold, and the rest had 90 seconds to create something for them to drink, down in one, from a 100ml glass – the food processor was allowed. First, it was harmless things: carrots, celery, tomatoes and a hint of spirits, which being poor students was either cheap vodka, cheap whisky or cheap tequila. Inevitably, there was always more than 100ml made and the rest was kept in the processor as a base for the next drink. The concoctions became more and more disgusting. After a while, male bravado and alcohol took over the job of reasoning. We all wanted a go and dispensed with the knife spinning. Spices were added, pasta sauces, plant leaves, marmite, uncooked lentils. Quite how our stomachs did not complain earlier I do no know. But then Miles, knowing how much I hate cucumbers, added half of one into the mixer, coupled with tequila, a teaspoon of vegetable stock, two squares of chocolate, ice and to try and disguise the smell, topped it all up with beer (he proudly informed me of this after the event). Normally I could smell cucumber or anything containing it a mile away. Here however, the glass was loaded into our left hand and ready for us to down in one.

The moment it started to slide down my throat, the aroma of cucumber came back up, invading my mouth. It was at that point it called for re-enforcements from the deep, only they had no plans to hang around in my mouth and wanted to join the party on the outside. The table was covered and after ripping off my blind fold, I surveyed the scene of carnage just long enough to catch a breath before adding to my offering, which was now moving across the table like ice-cold lava. The taste that remained in my mouth was not one of vomit, but of cucumber. Still to this day, the sight and smell of a freshly cut cucumber severely tests my constitution.

"So what did the specialist say about your allergies then?"

"She said I had candida and needed to give up yeast. Funny, I've met three other people who have been to her since, one of whom is just a rich kid with nothing better to spend his money on and certainly no allergies. She told them all they have varying forms of candida. We think she is some kind of cult leader. Her religion is a yeast-free diet and she will not stop until she has rid the world of fungus and fermentation."

I had no idea how to respond appropriately to this comment and I just walked outside and collected another box instead. When I returned, Paul had disappeared, presumably into the office. Marie-Louise was serving someone, a man in his sixties with a worn black leather jacket, very well dressed underneath and half-rim glasses perched on the end of his nose. He looked not unlike I imagined a French poet would look.

I went back out to collect the last two boxes. They were slightly smaller in size and I decided I could handle them together. They were heavier in relation to the bigger boxes, but something manly in me was rising to the surface. I was approaching the door contemplating exactly how I was going to open it when the poet came to my rescue. He had ordered his drink to go and opened the door wide and stood back without a smile. I thanked him as I slipped past without a response. The delivery driver was immersed in a paper and I let him know his van was empty. He remained taciturn. Why was nobody able to register an appropriate response? I had been stacking the boxes at the back of the café and I asked Marie-Louise where she wanted them.

"Could you put them in the store room, please?"

"The store room?"

"Yes, at the back."

"The store room?"

"The middle door."

"That's a store room?"

"Yes. It should be unlocked."

I headed for the door as she started moisturising her hands. She recognised I might struggle to open the door without some assistance and came round to open it for me. It was a weighted door and she had to hold it open. There didn't look much room inside, but it could have been the dark. I heard her flip a switch.

"The light takes a while to come one."

I walked forward and I thought I felt something of her brush near my hand. The next thing I knew, my hand seemed to implode and pain shot through my body looking for somewhere to escape. I dropped the the boxes.

"Fuuuuuck!" The pain found its escape.

"Sorry Craig, sorry! What happened?"

"The fucking door slammed on my hand."

"Oh God, I am so sorry. My hands are still slippery and I let go of it."

I was cursing her a thousand times under my breath, but let none of them loose. Paul came out of his office, a flustered anti-hero due to his lack of speed.

"Who on earth was that?"

"It was Craig, I slammed the door on his hand by mistake."

The pain was starting to peak and I decided to punch one of the boxes to release it along with my emotions. The light suddenly flipped on and they both saw me take out my anger on the poor unsuspecting box. It split open, and bags of sugar were now tainted with my blood.

"Craig, you're bleeding!"

As Marie-Louise spoke, I looked at the blood and the door, and surmised my hand had caught the lock. A small part of skin was hanging off.

"Come with me, we have some plasters in the office. First, you can come to the toilet and I will clean this up. This is all my fault."

"Better to bleed in the sink than in the sugar. I'll clean this up. Don't want people to think blood is routinely kept in the store room." Paul said.

She led me into the toilet and cleaned off the blood under a cold running tap. I quickly forgot that it was her that let go of the door. Her hands were very softly massaging my hand and they felt oily with lotion. I looked at her face, but it was hidden under her hair. It hung between us like a stage curtain. As she looked up at me she hit a tender spot and once again, pain ran up my arm. I winced and this was the face she saw.

"I'm so sorry Craig. Can you forgive me?"

"It's fine." I felt this, but my face didn't show it and she went silent with guilt.

"If you come through to the office, I can clean it up and put a plaster on it."

The skin that was hanging off was still there and looked like it would survive. She wrapped my hand in a towel and led me through to the office opposite. The delivery driver had gone and the boxes still lay at the back of the café.

The first thing I noticed about the office was how narrow it was, like it had been stretched. Wooden shelving ran down the left-hand side at working height. Papers were strewn across the desks. On the other side of the office were filing cabinets and shelves, with half-full trays scattered over them. A couple of trade calendars adorned the walls and at least twenty post-it notes were dotted over any free surface area.

Marie-Louise opened one of the filing cabinets and pulled out a green plastic box with a white cross on it. She took out a plaster, a nondescript packet, a small roll of bandage tape and some scissors. She opened up the packet and I smelt alcohol.

"I think I owe you lunch myself after this."

She wiped the tissue over the wound, feeling like a dozen pin pricks. For a second, I felt like they had descended to my loins until I realised my phone was vibrating in my trouser pocket. I blushed, but she was thankfully unaware of all this. I put my hand into my pocket and surveyed the screen. It took a second to sink in that it was Kate calling me. I had been awaiting her call, but as I sat hand in hand with Marie-Louise, she was as close to unwelcome as possible. My thumb slid across the buttons and pressed the off one, firmly. After all I thought, I was low on battery and it might cut out any minute now. I will ring her back some other time.

"I'll have to take you up on that offer of lunch." I said, hoping that she had meant an invitation involving her, and not just the footing of a bill. It seemed like an unnatural silence, but I guess she was just concentrating on my hand. I decided to see if I could turn lunch into dinner that evening.

"Marie-Louise..."

"So, you ready to put those boxes in the store room yet?" Paul said as he burst through the door. "Everybody has sodded off after your antics. They think the show is over no doubt. Do bad things generally follow you around?"

I smiled in defeat.

"Putting the boxes away would cost you lunch and dinner."

"Fair enough, I was going to offer that anyway. Seriously though, don't worry about the boxes – we'll figure something out – but how about I buy you dinner tonight. There is a great curry place round the corner."

I looked at Marie-Louise. She was placing the plaster over my replaced skin flap as Paul hovered enthusiastically over us. It was far from romantic.

"Sounds like a good deal to me, Craig", she said.

"Yeah, I guess it does." I sighed. "What time do you finish up tonight then?"

Chapter 12

I didn't go to the doctor's in the end thinking he might look suspiciously at my hand and ask various probing questions. I would feel somewhat resentful at defending myself when someone was suggesting I was not taking care of my body and thought it might lead to further discussions about my family status and that was something I was reticent about.

I went home and changed and then met up with Paul for a curry. It was a dimly lit, cave of a restaurant, serving wonderful southern Indian cuisine and he generously repeated his offer of paying despite my protestations. When we had settled down, he took up the doctor's route.

"So where do your family live?"

"Bristol."

"You go back much."

"Not really."

"Problems?"

"You could say that." I said.

"You have any brothers or sisters."

"One brother."

"Me too, older. Yours?"

"Younger."

"Gee, you're a talker", he said.

"It's not something I feel that comfortable talking about."

"So tell me about it."

"Did you just hear what I said?"

"Yes, but the more you talk about it, the more comfortable it becomes."

"No, thank you."

"So is this to do with your brother or your folks?"

"Both."

"He's the favourite, huh?"

I was finding it increasingly difficult to stay calm. "You could say that."

"Because he was younger? Or did you go off the rails they laid down for you."

"If you must know, I stayed firmly on the rails, it was my brother who broke free."

"Sorry. What did he do?"

I dropped my nan, sighed and stared at him disapprovingly. I'm sure my face did not convey the anger I felt from within.

"Look, you can act all stoic if you want, but sooner or later you have got to let it out. That stuff will eat you up. You always stay so calm, I am not sure if you are on pills or what. You never seem to laugh a lot, you never seem to get angry. Where are your emotions?"

"Drugs." I said.

"You are taking drugs! From the doctor?"

"No, that's what my brother did. He is a drug addict."

"Why are they angry at you?"

"Because they are my friends...*were* my friends, that led him into that."

"I see."

"No, you don't see. You really can't see. You have no idea what it's like when you do everything to please people and then they are not satisfied. It happened with my brother, it happened with my parents, with Kate – nobody is ever satisfied with what I do, least of all me."

"So how did he get mixed up with your friends?"

Since I had sketched him the outline already, it seemed somewhat unfair to not finish the picture off. I feared he thought I had some part in my brother's slide.

"He's only a couple of years younger than me so we always hung around together. I guess when we got to 17, the others wanted to start experimenting a bit more. Alcohol got boring and repetitive and there is fuck all else to do where we were. I never wanted to join in. I guess my brother was always more adventurous than me. I think he felt a little like an outsider as he was younger, and that if he did that, they would accept him more."

Paul ordered another drink so as to occupy the space where I didn't speak. "I assume they accepted him more after that."

"Yeah, wholeheartedly. At first it was just marijuana, but soon they were going to clubs, popping pills. I hung out less and less with them, but the more I tried to part with them and take him with me, the closer he got to them. He always took it to an excess and they loved him for that. They promised me they would take care of him, but I knew no-one would hold him back, least of all me."

"And what did your parents say?"

"It all stared so slowly, that to begin with I just covered for him. I made up excuses all the time, and before I knew it, he was knee-deep in the scene and my parents had no idea. I heard rumours he was into harder stuff. Heard it from friends of friends. Of course, he was careful to hide that from me, and I never had the guts to ask him outright."

"But you must have noticed a change. Or your parents."

"They were kidding themselves. They just got angrier and angrier with me and then when Chris used to stay out, I used to tell them it was with my friends. They knew my friends, although they had no idea of what they were into. Then one evening, we were all out, he came back and ransacked the place. He took a rucksack, a bundle of clothes, all the money and jewellery in the house, and then just disappeared."

"What did your parents do?"

"I knew it was him, and said so. I explained about the trouble he was in, and everything that had been happening. They refused to call the police. They blamed me and told me I had to go and find him. 'Don't come back until you do' they said."

"Wow, how did you deal with that!"

"Not easily. I went and called on my friends. None of them knew where he was, or if they did, wouldn't tell me. Said he was hanging out with a new girl and she was with a different crew."

"Did your parents let you come back?"

"They did, but there was always a wall between us. After three months, I decided I had to get out of there. I haven't been back since."

"But what about your brother?"

"I met him a couple of times. Once was in a pub at Christmas time. I tried to guilt him into contacting our parents. He sent them a Christmas card so I guess he still has some feelings left. I also met him at a party. That was four years ago. He looked so ill." A cloth of silence draped over the table. I waited for it to settle. "Maybe that's why I never laugh. Go ahead, tell me it's none of my fault and how I need to buck up."

"You got me. I am just sorry about the whole thing. I can't begin to imagine how you must feel about that. At least now I know how you ended up in London."

"I don't even like this city. It's just far enough away so I don't get reminded about any of that. I go back occasionally to see my folks. My mother tries to play happy families, but we all know it's a façade. After a day or so, they ask me if I have heard from Chris and when I say no, everyone loses their motivation. It's like bursting a balloon, and I always feel like the one with the pin."

"I promise, I won't bring it up again."

"Good. That's all your getting on that, next subject please."

After an awkward few minutes commenting on and trying all the food, the topics of conversation filtered back to normality and flitted all over the place: my studies, London, coffee, my job, his travels, who serves the best curry in North London.

Despite the difficulties of eating Indian with one hand, I had a great time. I began the evening wishing I was sitting opposite Marie-Louise, but found Paul very engaging. He has a way of drawing you in. He asked so many questions and it was not until the end of the evening, I realised I had done most of the talking. I would have felt guilty at having dominated the conversation, yet I had no idea at the time. I also had an overwhelmingly good feeling about myself when I left him that evening, and I hoped Paul would be at the café the next morning as I wanted to pick up from where we left.

Chapter 13

When I entered the café, I was greeted with a shock. Marie-Louise was leaning upright against the counter talking to Kate. My heart quickened as if starting it's own 100m sprint. They turned to me at the same time and I immediately feared that Kate had been sharing all my secrets and bad habits with Marie-Louise.

"Craig, 'ow is your hand?"

I stared down at my hand and realised it had grabbed the attention of all three of us. If I had realised it was going to receive so much scrutiny, I would have bandaged it with more care. As it was, it looked like I had just draped a tea towel over it and clipped it together with a safety pin.

"My word, what on earth have you done to your hand?" It felt nice, although strange to get sympathy from Kate. Maybe, for a second I forgot we had split up.

"A door closed on it."

"That is not exactly true, Craig. He is just being nice. I let go of the door and it slammed into his hand. It was bleeding quite badly yesterday."

"Where did this happen?" I sensed a little jealous curiosity coming through in her voice.

"Here in the café. I was helping out with a delivery yesterday."

"Oh, you work here now?"

"No, just helping out a friend." Marie-Louise smiled at the exact moment Kate looked at her. I could not have planned it any better.

"So what were you two just talking about?" I tried not to sound concerned. They both looked a little confused.

"Nothing in particular. A little about France, and why Mary moved here." Another person who could not get her name right!

"It's Marie: Marie-Louise." I said.

"Oh, do forgive me. I am just awful with names."

"It's no problem, it happens a lot."

No it isn't all right, I thought. The least people should do is to be able to remember a person's name when given it.

"Would you like a coffee Craig?" Marie-Louise asked.

"Yes, please." I turned to Kate. "So what brings you here"

"It seemed as good a place as anywhere. Last time we met here."

"Yes, but we were planning to meet that time. I didn't know you were in the habit of going to cafés on your own." I said it as if it was something you would never catch me doing.

"As I didn't get the opportunity to arrange a place with you, it was the first place that came to my mind."

I looked at her quizzically. We were obviously talking at cross purposes.

"What do you mean, 'arrange a place with me'? We didn't talk."

"Yes, I know, that is the reason I left the message."

"Message?" At this point, a realisation evolved like spying an approaching train arriving from your platform. It seemed to take an age and no amount of willing it on would speed it up. "On my phone?"

"Where else would I leave a message for you?"

"I haven't checked it."

"I did send it yesterday afternoon. I said if you don't respond to the message, I would assume it was fine to meet and I would be here at eleven." I remembered the phone call from Kate when Marie-Louise was dressing my hand.

"I think you phoned just as I hurt my hand yesterday."

"Do you not check your messages?"

"I was out last night with a friend." I was quite pleased that there was enough going on in my life to forget to check my phone. I also felt quite bad, as if I was telling Kate I didn't care at all. "Sorry, I forgot."

"There is no damage done, you are here. Is it convenient to talk now?" Her upper class accent and the word 'convenient' made it seem more like arranging a board meeting.

"Fine." I wanted to meet her, but I didn't want to do it under the spotlight of Marie-Louise, who then pushed my coffee to me over the counter and refused to accept payment.

"It is the least I can do after hurting your hand yesterday."

When we sat down at the table, I noticed Donna and Matt were also in the corner. Matt pointed his finger in my direction in a gun shape to acknowledge me. I nodded back.

"She seems like a lovely girl. And she appears to like you."

I was awash with emotions: irritability, attentiveness, jubilance and melancholia. I also wanted to know what she meant by Marie-Louise appearing to like me, but I was dammed if I was going to ask her. I decided to just ignore the statement, which probably spoke volumes on its own. I reached for the sugar, deciding to try it again. I wondered if I would notice a difference this time.

"You are drinking sugar in your coffee now?"

"It's something I'm trying."

"In the whole time I have known you, you have never drunk coffee any other way than straight black. And the amount of times you lectured me on my flavoured drinks."

"OK I admit it. I am somewhat hypocritical."

"Do you like it that way?"

"Being hypocritical?"

"The sugar."

"It's all right actually."

"How about trying some caramel in that?" She looked at me over her latte and I could see in her eyes she was smiling.

"If you have some in your bag, I'm game."

"Oh, actually..." She picked up her bag and opened the zip. The smile was wiped from my face like an Etch A Sketch. I was about to construct some protest when she started laughing. "I couldn't resist. I can't believe how worried you looked at the thought of caramel." I let out a sigh of relief.

"So, why did you want to meet?" I was aware that I was continually on the aggressive with her and thought it about time I held off. "I'm sorry. How are you?"

"Quite well, thank you." She waited a few seconds and stared at her drink whilst stirring in way too much sugar. "I miss being able to talk to you. I really wanted to just sit down and enjoy a drink with you. There seemed a bit of an...emptiness without having you to talk to."

I was mildly surprised and gave a reflective pause.

"I know what you mean. There is quite a large gap in my life now."

"It seems like you have met a few nice people here."

"Yeah. It's a great little café. It's surprising how quickly you can come to feel at home with some people."

"I think I know what you mean."

"Kate, I have been a bit of a mess the last couple of weeks." She looked at me very seriously and I knew I had her full attention again. "I know I have not been acting very maturely. I really wish I could come up with something better than a cliché, but I really didn't know what I was missing until you left. I had started to take you for granted." All the while I was aware that Marie-Louise was in earshot, cleaning up, or moisturising her hands, but it didn't bother me that she might hear. "I am not suggesting anything, but I know I miss you. I miss having fun with you."

"I miss having fun with you too. And I could never imagine not having contact with you. You were not just my boyfriend, but a dear friend." She reached a hand across the table and placed it on mine. She smiled at me and we shared a moment. Our eyes held a gaze and for the first time in a week or so, I was reminded of the feelings that brought us together in the first place.

"How are things with your work? I popped in a couple of times, but could not see you", she said.

"I am still off sick."

"Sick! Because of your hand."

"No, depression. My doctor thinks I am depressed."

"I am sorry honey."

It is amazing how much a word can transform an entire sentence in meaning and interpretation. She hadn't called me honey for weeks. And we hadn't sat down without tension for that long either.

"It's not your fault. After all, there are a number of things in my life I want to address. Need to address. I realise I really can't stand that job. And that I had become so dependent on you. I think it put too much stress on you and the relationship. More of a burden."

"You were never a burden."

"Not in the strict sense of the word, but you must realise I had shut off so many corners of my life that you had become my life. Meeting these people here made me realise that I don't have any friends. One or two that I might catch up with once every six months, but I have shut Kim out for too long and there is nothing I regularly do for myself."

"Have you seen anyone recently then?"

"I saw Kim a couple of times. I think if I had another outlet for me, then you might not feel so pressured in the relationship. I think that is where I went wrong."

"Craig, you did not go wrong anywhere. I think you have just become a little too...negative. You give off this impression that you are angry with everything, and everyone."

"That's not true. I'm not angry at everything."

"Nevertheless, you give off this impression that you are not happy with things, especially not yourself. It's really hard to love someone who doesn't love himself, who doesn't find himself attractive. Sometimes you can be really bitter and resentful. I started to feel that bitterness too. Negativity breeds negativity, and I don't want to be a negative person."

I sensed she wanted to say something more. I refused to blink as it would set off a tear rolling down my cheek. I stared over her shoulder for a few seconds, observing the guy at the other front window table.

He was one of those people who could never look at the person he is talking to. He held the attention of a rather attractive looking 30 something, who seemed to hang on every word he said, but he looked around the room at everything except her as if he was merely recounting what he had eaten for breakfast. His scene played out as if he were some university professor expounding his knowledge on the needy and wanting. His disinterest spanned from the girl having nothing to offer him, and he was bored of people only wanting him for his superior intellect and vast knowledge.

I snapped back, aware our hands were still touching.

"You're right. I think you are right. I have no idea how I ended up like this. I don't like myself like this." My eyes started to sting. "Kate, can I ask you something?"

"I thought you might want to. Look, I am sorry about Gavin. I really handled that badly."

For a minute I had to think about who she meant.

"I assume Gavin is..."

"The man who helped me move. I really only wanted you to hear about him from me and not somebody else. However, I should have been more sensitive."

"I understand. If I had acted more maturely, I'm sure I would have recognised that. Bygones?"

She wriggled. She was gearing up to say something, but I beat her to it.

"Kate, move back in with me. What I mean is, I want you to keep your key. You don't have to come back just yet. We can step back for a bit and go slowly. You could just come over sometime and I could cook us a meal. Or we could go and see a film together, or a DVD at home." I realised that I had just collected all the snippets of idyllic scenarios we used to share together and offered all of them to her hoping she would pick one.

"Craig, I am not so sure that is a good idea."

"Of course. How about we just start with a simple meal together. Somewhere neither of us have been. We can just enjoy each other's company and see how we feel."

"Craig, I have started seeing Gavin."

My hopeful face that I pulled at the end of my proposal became set as if the wind had changed. Then it started to crumble.

"Eh?"

"I have started seeing Gavin. I thought I should tell you. I am really sorry to tell you, but you would find out at some point and I wanted you to know how much I still care about you."

"Eh?"

"I am moving in with him. This weekend."

"What?" I stared at her, dropped jaw for a long time, speechless.

"Craig, say something."

"What? What...what exactly do you want me to say?" I snapped my hands back.

"I realise you can't feel good, but really what could I do. I had to let you know."

"And really, is there anything I can possibly do or say that would change anything right now. Thank you once again, life. Just when I thought you were offering me a ray of light, the clouds part and drop a whole fucking ocean of shit on me."

I realised the impossibilities in this statement, but it is human nature to utter the most ridiculous things in times of high stress.

"Craig..."

"Could you just leave, please?"

"Craig..."

"Could you just *leave...please*?"

"No. I am not going to just walk out when we need to talk about this."

"Why do we need to talk about this? What can either of us possibly contribute at this point that would ease the situation in any way? You want one thing, I want another, and ultimately you will do what you want as it's your life and so once again I end up out in the cold. How long have we been split up? And you are already moving in with the guy!"

"But I don't want to stop seeing you."

"Well, you can look at a photograph then."

"I meant, I don't want to lose you as a friend."

"Do you seriously expect us to remain friends? Ask yourself if you could do that in my shoes. What is there for me in that friendship?"

"I can support you."

"Wonderful. Let's start planning it now then. I tell you what, I will come over at ten on Saturday morning and help you move. Then you can both take me out to dinner to say thank you. Better still, you can have me as your pet. You can let me sleep on the living room couch, feed me leftovers, take me out for walks in Finsbury Park and talk to me when the other one is pissing you off. Just don't forget to close the bedroom door at night or I might pop in the middle of you two having sex."

"I just thought..." the futility of talking rationally to me at this point seemed to suddenly dawn on her.

"Could you just leave, please?"

She got up, put on her jacket meekly, picked up her handbag and quietly re-placed the chair. She said sorry as she walked out.

I waited for her to clear the corner and then stormed out of the café in the opposite direction, the taste of sweet coffee tormenting my mouth.

Chapter 14

I spent a great deal of the next 24 hours in bed, drifting in and out of sleep, hopping from one bad dream to the next. In one, Kate was an elephant that I kept chained up in my flat. I spent a lot of time cleaning her feet with a toothbrush, and offering her buckets of water. For some reason, it was continually raining and we had leaks all over our apartment – even stranger since there was no roof on the flat. In another, she was running the London marathon without clothes and her body was covered in tattoos of previous boyfriends. I was running behind her, unable to keep up, and every time I could make out the name of a tattoo it read a different name. I had the feeling that if I was able to get in front of her, I would finally see the tattoo of me. Then the marathon crossed the Thames and I ran across a bridge, while the runners got in a boat. When I got to the other side, I could no longer see the boat. I never did see whether she had a tattoo of me. I remember one more in which Marie-Louise had turned into a flower in the café. She was placed on the counter where we order drinks and nobody had any knowledge of her. I kept trying to talk to her, but everybody thought I was crazy for talking to a flower. The flower needed watering and although I was aware of this, I felt too embarrassed to ask them to water her, for fear they would laugh at me. The flower started to resent me and flicked dirt in my coffee. Despite seeing the dirt go in my coffee, I still drank it. I never normally remember dreams.

When awake, I felt more confused. What I found most perplexing, was that she had been so indecisive with regards our relationship, but very decisive about moving in with Gavin. I tried to take a step back and view the situation objectively, with little success. I could not assess whether I was being out of line reacting to her and Gavin the way I did, or if I had some justification. I also felt foolish at having opened up to her and having it thrown back in my face. I needed to talk about the situation and also check that Marie-Louise was not a flower.

As I walked in, she was sitting on one of the high chairs at the back of the café with her arms folded on the table and her head sunk between them. She was stationary. I thought she was crying; it seemed like the sort of thing people would do in this pose. Paul came out of the office wiping his hands on a towel, looked at me and smiled. He whispered some words at me, which I initially thought might have been 'women's pain' until I realised this was most unlike Paul. He turned the volume up a little when he realised I missed the first broadcast – 'migraine'.

"Oh, how long for?"

"About half an hour. I told her to go home, but she wanted to see if it passed. Said she didn't want to let me down."

"Do you want me to try and have a word with her?" A disproportionate amount of faith in my ability to talk sense in to her swelled within me. Paul didn't seem surprised.

"Feel free, I think it's getting worse. She would be no use here anyway."

I walked up to her as though I was planning to surprise her with a loud 'BOO'. Quite why I wanted to creep up on her I do not know. I reached out my hand and kept it in mid-air above her shoulder, thinking better of the idea to place it there at the last second. I pulled myself up alongside her with my hand in the same place, as if I were performing some mime.

"Hi, Marie-Louise. Paul says you have a migraine."

She looked up and her hair fell all over her face. She looked like she had just woken up. Normally, I would have been tempted to laugh at her look.

"Hi Craig". She looked back down again. "Sorry, I can't stand the light at the moment." Her muffled speech created distance between us.

"Don't you think it's better to be at home rather than here at the moment? Paul doesn't need you today and it looks as if the place is dead."

"Hmm."

"Does that mean you'll go home?"

"Hmm."

I really wasn't sure what this meant.

"Does that mean yes?"

"Hmmokaaayy."

I thought in the middle of all the hair I had heard an OK. I wasn't going to push her more as she was clearly in pain. I walked back over to the counter as a masculinely built female came through the door.

"She's agreed to go home...I think. I don't think she should go home alone, so I can take her to the bus stop"

"I think a taxi is better." I cursed myself that Paul's idea was better than mine.

Man-woman walked straight past the counter, behind me and over to Marie-Louise. She draped her arms over Marie-Louise and started talking to her in French. Why didn't I do that? Not the French bit, but the rest of it was quite possible. And now she would have been so thankful that Craig was there to take care of her. I was angry with my diffidence.

"Who's that?" I turned and asked Paul.

"No idea! I've never seen her before."

She turned back and walked towards us. She spoke with confidence and a far stronger accent than Marie-Louise.

"Listen, she got to go home, she said you says this was OK?"

"I've been trying to get her to go home for ages now, so if you can persuade her, you're in my good books."

Hang on I thought! I just persuaded her to go home and now this charlatan was coming in and stealing my thunder. I was just about to speak when she turned to us both.

"So you must be Paul and you must be Cregg." She made my name like a type of rock. The good news however, was that if she knew my name, Marie-Louise must have mentioned me.

"Correct, and you are?" Paul offered out his hand.

"Laura."

"Pleasure to meet you Laura." She handed Paul her hand and then rounded to me. I felt compelled to give her my side of the story.

"Hi. Marie-Louise just agreed to go home and we said she should get a taxi and I would make sure she got home safely. Do you want to come as well?" I figured Paul would not contradict me seeing as he was stuck here now anyway and seemed somewhat taken with Laura.

"Oh, that is no a problem. I can drive her home with my car."

Paul replied annoyingly quickly.

"That works out well because I could do with a hand here at the moment, if you are not too busy Craig?"

I sighed. I don't know why I was so desperate to see her. After all, if I wanted to talk about what happened with Kate, I should feel much more comfortable talking to Paul about it.

"Yeah, no problem." I had a defeated look on my face. Laura said this was wonderful and hoped to meet us again soon. As a parting shot, she extended her arm and placed her right hand on my left upper arm and ruffled my cashmere jumper. I felt like a son being praised by his mother. Then she was off to Marie-Louise and started to help her up from her chair. I turned to Paul who was staring in Laura's direction.

"So what do you want me to do?"

"Hmm?"

"What do you want me to do?" It was the first time I felt like I was the wise one whilst talking to Paul.

"Hmm?" At least this time he was looking at me. His attention snapped back. "Oh, well I still have to place an order which will take half an hour, only it's got to be placed pretty soon. Have you ever made coffee before?" I had plenty of experience with a cafetiére but zero with a professional machine.

"Of course I have. What kind of question is that? Just not espressos."

I'm not sure if my resentment shined through. He gave me an overview on making an espresso, to which I paid close attention. First, he emptied the filter of the dregs, which he hit down on the metal drawer with so much force, it demonstrated how cafés aren't completely peaceful: all manner of beats ring out in percussive harmony. The driving rhythm of coffee filters being banged empty is accompanied by a high tempo of spoons on saucers, a riff of coffee percolating and fills of intermittent steam sprays. All this is accompanied by a lead vocal of chatter and gossip. It seems amazing people go to a café to think! After showing me how to fill the filter and attach it to the machine, it all seemed so easy. He then showed me where he kept the beans for the cafetiéres. He had five different roasts in ascending order of strength: Midday, Vienna, Yin-Yang, French, and Midnight.

"Help yourself to a drink, I assume you want one. And then if you could man the fort for a while. I'll be over here in case you need me. If anyone wants something fancy just give me a shout." Since this coffee was on the house, I decided to try the Midday roast.

While my coffee was brewing, I acquainted myself with the nooks and crannies behind the counter. As I opened the drawer of used coffee, a waft of air came up somewhere between coffee and stale cigarettes and it was the first time I had found the smell of coffee unpleasant. Still, I started to feel quite comfortable. True, I wasn't up to cappuccinos, but I could hope that everyone ordered black coffee or tea and I would be fine. My first customer was Bobby K.

"Hey, check out Craig the man here." I wasn't sure if this was a nickname or an observation. "How long you been working here?"

I checked my watch.

"About eight minutes. What can I get you?"

"Let me see." His eyes darted up to the board and I could swear he was scanning for the most complex drink to make.

"He'll have what he always has: a normal white coffee, and he can pour his own cream." Paul spoke without lifting his head from his orders.

"Er, yeah stimmt."

"Sorry?" I said.

"White coffee."

"Cafetiére or espresso?"

"Espresso, bro.'"

It almost seemed like he was trying out various nicknames on me to find out which one I disliked the most. He needn't have put so much effort in, seeing as how whatever he called me I was uncomfortable with. I noticed his cards again. He started to fiddle with them, while I limply banged out the used coffee from my filter. Some was still stuck in the corner like a petrified child refusing to come out from under the bed. Paul looked over at me and mouthed the word 'harder'. I complied and so did the coffee, unfortunately complete with the filter, which dropped into the used coffee. Great start Craig! Ordinarily I would have washed it out after fishing it out, but seeing as how it was Bobby K, I brushed off the visible grains and used it as it was. I put the coffee on the go and realised I had no idea how much it cost. I barely realised how much I paid for mine normally.

"That's..."; I swivelled my head up and round to the price board, studying it as though it were an incoming aeroplane; "...one-eighty please, sir". I looked down and saw there was already two pounds on the counter.

"Put the over in Miss Piggy. Cool pig!" he threw in the direction of Paul. I was glad he complimented my taste and it gave me greater pleasure that he didn't even realise it. I was not going to tell him it was my choice of pig.

"So you taken this up full-time?" His question was pitched somewhere between intrigue and boredom.

"Why? You want the job instead?"

"You interviewing now?"

"You applying?"

I realised this was a fruitless exercise. Quite why I had taken a disliking to him I could not remember, but it was time I tried to reverse this. A smile is always a good start.

"Actually, I am just helping Paul out. Marie-Louise went home sick, but I do actually have a secret plan to take over the place."

"I been trying for a while," added Bobby K, "but he's never let me behind there before. Maybe we could team up on him."

We had both raised our voices in the hope that Paul would hear, but he seemed helplessly engrossed in his orders. I tried again.

"I'll empty the till, you open your bag and then make a run for it."

"All right, but smartish. The 29 comes in a minute and that's my getaway. Meet you in Traf Square at six."

"Ha, bloody ha. You think I am not paying attention, but I hear all that goes on. Go ahead, steal all you want. Not much there anyway."

The atmosphere lightened and I wondered if Bobby K's personality was like a mirror. He often reflected back whatever behaviour you threw in his direction. He walked over to Paul, chatted seriously for five minutes then headed for the door, waving as he went past.

"Enjoy, Craig. Careful, this is how Thomas started here years ago, now he can't leave." I cast a frozen smile over the café.

Over the next 40 minutes I had five more customers: two for espressos; one for white coffee; one for tea; and one for cappuccino, which Paul came over and made. These were accompanied by two cakes: one coffee and walnut, and one mandarin cheesecake. I started to think that this was something I could get quite into. It was sociable, not too taxing and no stress. Unlike selling, where you have targets and people come to you for advice, here the customers always know exactly what they want.

Paul finished his order, faxed it off, and then came and relieved me. He offered me a tenner for the hour, but I told him this was ridiculous.

I was there anyway and with Marie-Louise absent, concentrating on customers – or lack of – gave me something to focus on. He said that next time I was in he would pay for my coffee and cake and I agreed it was a fair trade off.

As I was drying my hands readying to leave, I realised I had completely forgotten what had brought me there in the first place. Despite having spent most of the previous 24 hours thinking of only Kate, the last hour I had been relieved of this burden. I considered bringing it up with Paul, but as he was on his own, it was unfair to ask him to give me his full attention. As I walked away from the café, I didn't feel so weighed down with thoughts of Kate. I hoped the feeling would last.

Chapter 15

I sighed when she asked me about Kate. It was an automatic reaction and not meant towards her, but I think she missed this. I didn't want to talk about it partly because I had a fear of being honest with myself. Whatever attraction I had towards Marie-Louise, would never be reciprocated if I had to admit that I still wanted to be with Kate. I also had no idea what I was going to say and that frightened me too.

"Did she do something wrong?" Marie-Louise asked.

"No, not exactly."

"Did you do something wrong?"

I stopped to think of something that I had done wrong. The pause was obviously misinterpreted by Marie-Louise as an admission of guilt.

"Were you interested in other women?"

Again I thought about it.

"You know, I thought I might be. I thought a couple of times it might be cool to be at the beginning again, with the spark and the sex, and you don't have to work at anything because it all seems so natural. But whenever I actually read about it, or saw it in a film, it sapped all the excitement out of it. It was as if I liked to dream about it in the perfect sense, but as soon as I was faced with realities, it shut me down. I realised I was happy with her, just unhappy with the situation. I guess everyone gets a bit like that. I just didn't have any sexual attraction to anyone but her – a bit of a bummer if your thinking about having an affair."

Was my attraction to Marie-Louise because she showed none towards me and therefore I could paint the idea of a perfect affair onto her? What would I do if she showed me some interest? Then, I really would have to choose between Kate or her, even though at the moment there was no Kate and there was no attraction from Marie-Louise.

"So you didn't do anything wrong?"

"No. I don't think so." Was I to blame? When Kate said she was not happy with me, I might have wanted her back just to be in control. Then again, I think most relationships are about some form of control, not necessarily conscious, but certainly sub-conscious. When you are in a committed relationship, certain things are expected of you. We realise that certain behaviour is just naturally unacceptable: spending all the other persons money, sleeping with someone else, bringing a pet monkey into the flat without asking the other person. These things are never discussed, just given.

Problems come in a relationship when there are things which fall on the boundary of acceptability and are either discussed or just accepted for a quiet life. Things such as staying out late most nights of the week with your friends, wanting to go on holiday to a particular place, or whether you leave the lid to the toothpaste on or off. If they are accepted for a quiet life, then one person is controlled even if the other person is unaware of this. If there is a discussion then either a satisfactory compromise is made or someone gives in. You can't compromise on everything and when someone gives in, this is control.

I fall mostly into the quiet life category, and in that way, Kate had a great deal of control over me. She often stayed out late and drank with friends. She brought a lizard into our life without me having a say in it: 'It just sits in a tank and does nothing, you won't even have to feed it' she said. To which I replied 'why not buy a bit of wood?'. And yes she did often leave the toothpaste lid off, which really bugged me. In the beginning, when everything was love and roses, I just accepted it as one of her adorable quirks. But after a while, it began to bother me, and by the time we reached the rumblings of war it was too late. I mentioned it a couple of times like a joke and she resented me 'always making fun of her' and so I gave up and just accepted it – control.

And after we split up, the control continued. It was her that wanted to sleep in separate bedrooms. Why? She said she was considering whether she still loved me, but when she went out and got drunk with her friends, she crawled back into our bed at night wanting sex. Then when she woke in the early hours, she would get a glass of water and transfer into the living room. She chose when to see me, I never asked to see her. I'm sure one of the reasons I was so pissed off was I had lost control of my life and I was either being coerced what to do at work or coerced what to do at home.

I realised that as scrappy and disorganised as the last two weeks had been, at least I had had control over it: no boss with snide remarks; no targets to fulfil; nobody unhappy with me because I wasn't fulfilling their expected behaviour; and no toothpaste smell in the bathroom. Staring at the home-made cakes, I unconsciously added to my answer;

"And she didn't do anything wrong either. It was just a bad fit."

"How long were you together?"

"Two years." I noticed that she was moisturising her hands again. It was the first time I had grouped all the times I had seen her do this together. I also noticed a slight red patch peaking out from behind her collar on the left side of her neck. The patch kept popping up from behind her collar as she moved, as if coming up for air.

"Wow, that's a long time."

The mood was silenced by the crash of a saucer on the floor. I half expected to turn and see Donna standing over the evidence and waving her tissue in triumph. Instead, I saw Jam Man, with a jam smeared spoon in one hand, a muffin in the other, and his plate in pieces at his feet. He was nonplussed, looking like an archaeologist finding Roman remains in New York City. Marie-Louise went to clear it up and Jam Man looked at me protesting his innocence. I frowned back, in no mood to make other people feel better.

When she came back to the counter, she offered to buy me a drink. I also asked for a slice of coffee and walnut cake, counting out the money on the counter.

"So what about you and your boyfriend?"

"Oh, we split up." There was a lilt in her voice, suggesting everything was not completely in order.

"Really. Recently?" Did I sound happy?

"About two weeks ago."

"What went wrong?"

"Well, he started spending a lot of time with this other woman. I didn't like that, so I told him and he didn't seem happy with what I said."

"And he broke up with you because of that?" She seemed unable to get her words out. "You don't have to talk about it if you don't want to."

"I think it might do me good to talk about it." Two guys came in: a black man with a build like a sideways-squashed bowling ball and an emaciated white man in very baggy clothes that looked as if he had spent the month in them. They ordered their drinks, and the white guy noticed me standing there. He greeted me with a strong Welsh accent, then they went over to the window seat where I had sat on my first day here, pulled out several scraps of paper and started writing.

"So is, sorry was, your boyfriend French?"

"Yes, I met him in Paris. We were together while I lived there, but we decided that when I went to England it would be too difficult to continue, so we said we would be free from each other for a while and see how it went. Then, a few months ago, I needed to get out of London and decided to travel around. We spoke on the phone and he said he felt like a semester off, so we went around together and started seeing each other again. When we came back to London, he had a friend who worked in a pub near Hyde Park and they gave him a room and a job. They said I could stay as well, but they only had one job. After two weeks, another staff member left and they asked if I could work there."

"And did you?"

"Well, yes. I needed a job somewhere and it meant I could stay with René for longer." I squirmed that he had a name now. "Things were fine, but the landlady said that she found it disruptive for couples to work together. It was not a problem, but meant we saw less of each other."

"How did he feel?"

"He seemed fine with it. But then I noticed I never worked with the landlady and she always worked with René. I think I was a little jealous, but then I heard that a previous member of staff had left because the landlady started to...want, or demand things from him."

"Demand what? Work shifts?"

"No, *things*." She paused and when it became clear the penny was not going to drop, she sighed. "Sexual things."

"Oh!" Then it hit me. I wasn't thinking and just mumbled, "Lucky guy!"

"What?"

"Um, why?"

"I was told she was always doing this. That it had happened lots before."

"Who told you this?"

"Djemal. He was René's friend who got him the job. Djemal and me worked most of the shifts together as René was with the landlady."

"What did you do about it?"

"I told René he had to stop working with her."

"Did he say she had tried something with him?"

"Well, no. But he refused to stop working with her."

"And you were not happy with this I guess?" I realised I was doing nothing but ask questions and I didn't want to make her feel like she was on the spot.

"No, I wasn't. He said I needed to trust him, but after the things she did, and when he refused to change shifts, I knew there was something going on."

I paused. I didn't want to offer up a sixth question in a row and yet something seemed a little odd. This was also the first conversation where she had let me into her world and I didn't want to upset her by saying she may have been hasty. My silence was not a good answer.

"Why are you looking at me like that? You haven't said anything."

"No reason, I'm just listening."

"But you don't agree, no? I can tell you don't agree with me."

My pauses were becoming longer and louder. It was obvious I would have to explain myself.

"I am just not sure what he did wrong. What did you do next?"

It was her turn to pause now.

"Well, I really thought there was something going on and so I decided to talk to the landlady about it. She was so rude! She said I was a spoilt little child and that she was not interested in René and if I had a problem then I should talk to him about it." Inside, I agreeingly nodded my head; outside, I did all I could to keep it still. My silence was as good as an encouragement for her to carry on.

"When I told this to Djemal, he said they were both out of order." She began to shift on the spot as if trying to wriggle free of something. Her speech had slowed a little and became more deliberate. "He said I needed to get away from it all and that we should go out, a change of scenery. This seemed like a good idea and we went to a restaurant near where he lives. I said I was afraid to go back to the pub as the landlady may have spoken to René or done something to make me feel really uncomfortable. Djemal said I could stay at his." I had a pretty good idea at what was coming. "Djemal said he would not let me sleep on the sofa and I wouldn't let him give up his bed so I said we should share the bed. Then he told me that he thought I deserved better than René. I really didn't want anything, I mean it was not something I tried to provoke, but René had been so unreasonable." She admitted they had sex.

"What happened next?"

"When I got back to the pub in the morning, I had twenty minutes before my shift and René was waiting for me. He asked where I had been the night before. I said I needed to clear my head. I lied and said that Rita, the landlady, had shouted at me and I didn't feel comfortable. I just couldn't look him in the eye. He said he had no idea about Rita, but felt bad about me feeling bad and thought we should look for a different job. He had covered our bed with flowers. If he had just listened to me in the first place..."

I felt depleted. I knew she would ask me what I thought, and I felt her actions were very immature. Then I thought about how I had dealt with Kate and decided to ease off on my judgement, but sure enough, her question came.

"I moved out into Djemal's until I found another place, but made it clear what had happened was a mistake. I told René I thought maybe we were not right for one another. Do you think I should have told him about Djemal?"

"You didn't tell him about Djemal?" I don't think I could have injected more shock into my voice if I tried. "Marie-Louise, at this moment he might be thinking he was completely to blame."

"Well, he was, partly."

"What do you mean? He refuses to stop working with someone who you had heard rumours about being a man-eater. Rumours I might add, from someone who wanted to sleep with you. And then you have no evidence whatsoever that something went on, or that the landlady was even interested. And how about trusting your boyfriend? After all, trust should be the basis of any relationship. And even if everything else was true, which it wasn't, it doesn't say much about your feelings for René that you go off and sleep with the next guy that comes along." I think I threw that line in there because I was hoping I might be the *next* next guy. Or I was referring to Kate and Gavin. Either way, it was an awful use of wording and I was appalled at myself for my outburst. Why didn't I just agree with everything she said? At least then I would be the new friend who understands. I didn't want to get drawn in, but I had already wandered in too far.

"What do you mean no evidence? Most men given half the chance would sleep with another woman if he thought he could get away with it. And even more so if they gave him a job, place to stay and, I don't know – maybe a pay rise."

"Listen to yourself. 'Maybe' a pay rise, 'place to live' and 'job'. I assume the word 'maybe' means you don't have a clue if this is true. And a place to live and a job are not benefits: you have to work in return for money, and pay for the place to live. And I completely resent the suggestion that all men want an easy fuck. I certainly have never done anything like that, even though it happened to me, twice. Whatever happened to talking about problems? Relationships deserve a bit of hard work, it's not all sex and candy."

I held back the last sentence a little. I realised I had crossed a line. My own frustration at having been on the receiving end before had left a scar. Now I was poking at it and directing my own anger at Marie-Louise. I could hardly bear to think about what she thought of me now. As she stood looking at me, it was the first time I thought that she looked really vulnerable.

I felt I had outstayed my welcome. I mumbled, stuttered, and shuffled on the spot, and then decided to excuse myself.

"I should...probably...get going. I guess you have things to do." I turned to the door and slowly started my exit. I suddenly noticed the other people in the café had all gone quiet. I wasn't sure how long they had been listening, but only deaf customers would have failed to hear my speech. I didn't know who they sided with, or if they expected me to leave. I turned back one last time.

"Listen, sorry. I really didn't mean to..." but I wasn't sure what else to add to that. After all, I did mean what I said. I left the café, like a defeated boxer leaving the ring.

Chapter 16

I considered staying away from the café the next afternoon. I was aware that Marie-Louise was supposed to have the day off, but with Thomas being ill, this could have changed. I decided upon a cowardly approach of walking past the café on the other side of the road in some rarely worn clothes to see if I could spy her. The ludicrousness hit me when I displayed anger at a parked van I had been hiding behind, as it drove off leaving me exposed. Skulking around the lamppost opposite, I only saw Paul bent over the counter reading a newspaper. Paul was a self-confessed, half-hearted Guardian reader; he wanted to read a newspaper and decided upon the Guardian as the best of a bad bunch, but was not fully committed to either choice.

I risked an entrance. I banked on Marie-Louise not having talked to Paul about our argument, and thought I could find a way of letting him know without it sounding so bad. After all, it's not nice to tell someone whom you trust, and who trusts you, that you came in and shouted at his new employee in front of a full café.

As I entered he looked up and smiled affectionately – obviously he didn't know. Although it was nearly five in the afternoon, all of the tables were occupied. At my favourite window table sat the dice group. The same three girls often sat in that corner, played Yahtzee together, and drank cappuccinos. They always paused after a round to go outside and smoke a cigarette, before coming back and playing another. Paul did not insist that people smoke outside, rather, 'requested' it, and I had never seen anyone smoke inside. As they carried on rolling, I shakily made my way to the counter.

"Same as?" Paul said.

"Always. Looks quite busy today."

"Yeah, it's nice to have a full house. Especially when I get to go home in a couple of hours."

"Any plans for the evening?"

"Not yet. Tidy up my flat I guess."

"Entertaining over the weekend?"

"Not really. Well, kind of. My son is staying with me Saturday and Sunday night."

I found it hard to believe that we had been out for curry together and he failed to mention he had a child. I had never imagined this. I guess, when you always see people in the same place, it's hard to imagine them outside of that environment.

"How old is he?

"Nine. Soon to be ten."

"And what's his name?"

"Stefan."

"You never mentioned him before." I was proceeding slowly after yesterday's disaster discussing personal lives. "Do you see him often?"

"Usually every other weekend. I pick him up Saturday after work and have him until Monday morning when I take him to school."

"So do you have any plans with him, or are you just hanging out."

"I thought if the weather was nice we might head up to Hampstead Heath with a picnic. He's got a kite he loves flying."

"Does he ever come to the café?"

"He's been here with his mum once or twice, but generally I'm either working, or the café is closed, so not often."

I searched for another topic to talk about, but his phone started ringing. I was kicking around the idea of telling him about the argument when it became clear, from his side at least, the phone call was unwelcome news. I tried my best to look like I wasn't paying attention, but with no food or drink, no table, and no book, there was only so much I could stare at. Except for the dice group, there was only one other person I had seen before, the lady on the table directly behind where I stood. She looked the professional type: an all grey suit and shiny white shirt with an oversized collar. Despite being obviously tall, her shoulders, neck and head seemed to have been recklessly crammed into her frame. She had straight, almost flat, blonde hair. It looked as if gravity was working overtime to pull her entire upper torso towards the ground and this had contributed to her bad posture.

She was writing a text message and occasionally jolting back with suppressed laughter. It reminded me of when doctors try to bring back flatliners to life with shock pads. I had seen her once or twice, coming as I was going or vice versa. She looked up from her mobile, smiled at me, said hello and went back to her message. I felt awkward. It really unnerves me when strangers say hello to me. Maybe it's the result of living in London for so long, but there is an unspoken rule that strangers never greet each other in cities. It's a rule sandwiched between 'never make eye contact with strangers' and 'if someone drops down unconscious in the middle of the street; move along'. The latter I had witnessed that afternoon on the way to Camden.

I had decided to take the tube instead of the bus. I and three others crowded around the door and when no-one got off, we stepped on. In the centre of the standing section where you enter the tube, was an old man, lying on the floor. His clothes looked like Yoko Ono had recently taken a pair of scissors to them in the name of art, and his face was so full of blemishes and without colour, it reminded me of the surface of the moon. An almost visible odour emanated from him, attacking our nostrils and as we stepped on; we all tip-toed around him. Nobody looked directly at him, as if he were something to avoid stepping in, instead of on. Then we all sat down and nobody looked in his direction. At the next stop, everyone got off through the other doors and I realised now why the carriage was empty.

I could not take my mind off him though. Had anyone checked to see if he was breathing? How long had he been there? Had someone been alerted? I started to think about what I could possibly do. There was no underground worker in this carriage. Come to think of it, I couldn't remember ever seeing an underground worker in a carriage. In fact, if you had a problem on the train, how the hell were you supposed to let people know? There was an emergency brake, but this would just result in an angry mob itching to jump you for making them late, and a fine from the underground for unnecessarily stopping the train. What exactly does warrant an emergency brake?

I stared at the man, hoping for signs of life. I looked around. I couldn't stand the thought of being so unconnected to someone that I would fail to realise they were dead.

"Excuse me," I said.

The train pulled to a halt and I realised it was my stop. Without pausing to think, I sprang in the direction of the closing door and just managed to squeeze through. I breathed a sigh of relief, until I noticed something about the man had stayed with me – more than just his smell. At this point I decided to do something about it. I went and found an elusive underground worker upstairs in the station.

"Excuse me, could you help me? There was an unconscious man on the train I was just on, and I wanted to report him."

"Did he assault you in some way, mate?" I found his immediate resort to the word 'mate' to be an indication that he was not altogether sympathetic to my report.

"No, no. He was just lying there unconscious. For all I know he was dead."

"You want to report a dead man on the tube?"

"No, no, he wasn't dead. At least I don't think, or rather hope he wasn't. He could have been sleeping."

"And what did he do to you, that makes you want to report him."

"Nothing, he was just lying there."

"Aha. And this annoyed you did it, *mate*." He was starting to annoy me with his inability to grasp my story.

"No, it didn't annoy me. I just wanted to make sure he was all right. Not dead, like."

"So what happened when you checked him?" I stared a little over his shoulder wondering why I ever thought this was the humane thing to do. I'm sure no-one else bothered to mention him to anyone.

"I didn't check him. I didn't want to..." I couldn't think of how to finish the sentence that might clarify things for the man, and keep my dignity intact.

"Oh, I see. You didn't want to wake him from the dead? Well, that's very considerate of you."

"Look there was a man lying on the floor on an underground carriage. I got on at Archway and he was already lying there. He didn't move in the whole of the journey to Camden, and when I got off he was still there. There were no underground workers around for me to report...*tell* about him, and you were the first person I saw."

"I am sorry there were no other workers around, *sir*." I think I preferred mate. "All the rest of my colleagues are out in the parks checking to see if the other bums are alive and well. They carry around Thermos flasks full of hot chocolate for them you know. You could join them if you like. We are always on the lookout for volunteers. Oh no, that's right – you don't want to disturb them. Never mind, *sir*. Rest assured they will get round to him eventually. In the meantime, thank you for your help and we'll get right on it. Have a nice day, *sir*."

He walked over to the door leading to the ticket office and left me paralysed. I couldn't believe what had just happened. Sometimes, I feel I would be quite happy to never see another human as long as I live.

Anyway, the woman behind me in the café had just violated the 'don't talk to strangers' law, and now I was unnerved. I thought about leaving it at that, but instead, glutton for more punishment, decided to take action.

"Excuse me, is anyone sitting here?" I pointed at the chair opposite as I could see that Paul was busy trying to sort out some problem over the phone.

"No, please, go ahead."

As soon as I pulled the chair back, I noticed the name tag on her suit was from my workplace.

KARINA BROWN
SALES ASSISTANT

A shiver went up my spine for the second time that afternoon. I had just pulled up a chair next to a work colleague of mine! I had not made her acquaintance yet, so she must have started since I had been off, and here I was, sitting with her in a café, while I was off sick with depression. In retrospect it was a bad idea, but I felt the need to talk.

"Do you come here often?" This must be the most unimaginative line someone can come up with to start a conversation, on a par with 'been busy?', when you jump in a late night taxi.

"Quite often, it's so convenient isn't it?"

"Is it?"

"Well, yeah. It's so close."

I realised my cover was blown. "Yeah, I guess it is. So how long have you worked for..."

"About three weeks. Well, only a couple in store, I had to do the training course for a week."

"Still in Leicester is it?"

"That's right. How long ago did you do it?"

"Oh, about ten years or so, I've lost track now."

"Were they very patronising back then?"

"Yeah, nothing changes there. You just have to swallow what they feed you and wait for it to come back up. It's not long before you start developing your own style."

"How long are you on holiday for?"

I was relieved to avoid explaining why I was depressed and hanging out in cafés. I assume my manager wanted to save face or, if I felt like being positive, felt a little sorry for me and wanted to save my face.

"At the moment I am not sure. I have a lot of holiday left over from last year and it's not so busy this time of year. Sorry, but how did you know I work there? I am sure I've been off since you started."

"I think it was your last day. I came in late in the afternoon to introduce myself again to the manager and he needed a few details. I saw you on the shop floor. I was going to introduce myself, but someone told me you were very unhappy that day as your girlfriend had split up with you."

Jesus! Couldn't anyone keep a secret?

"So how is it, still using the Perfect Loop?" She chuckled. The Perfect Loop meant the line 'It's Perfect, isn't it?' It is the line we should use to close every sale, and is supposed to allow you to identify every eventuality of negative response the customer may have which you can then overcome. In reality, it is just a security method, so if you choose to think for yourself and not use it, and your sales are bad, they have an excuse to fire you.

"Yeah. I still feel a little self-conscious using it, but I find it quite useful. I had good sales this week. Over 100% of target and still have tomorrow to go."

I am sure my boss loves her. Apart from making targets, she has long legs and is not afraid to show them. I'll bet he makes her go up ladders to clean TVs, and stands at the bottom staring up at them. I was imagining this image when I was suddenly interrupted by Paul.

"Hey Craig. I know this is starting to sound like I am taking the piss, but any chance I can ask a favour of you?"

"Go ahead."

"Well, I have a bit of a crisis going on. My ex wants to change things around this weekend as she is going away on holiday." I was surprised by how he was willing to share this with Karina as well. "Anyway, now she wants to go away with Stefan Saturday and so I can't have him tomorrow night. But if I want to, I can have him tonight. Trouble is, I am supposed to be opening up with Marie-Louise in the morning at seven. There's no way I can have Stefan and get here that early. I was wondering if you could possibly cover for me in the morning for a couple of hours so I could have Stefan tonight. You won't have to work too hard as she knows the ropes, but you can just hang around and help out with the heavy stuff. I'll pay you of course."

How would Marie-Louise react? I was sure if he phoned and asked her, she would not come into work.

"Are you going to ask Marie-Louise if she minds?"

"She'll be fine. I don't really want to disturb her on a day off. Besides you both get on well, I'm sure she'll be relieved to see you instead of me turning up."

I was tempted to help him out and certain she would say something to him if he phoned and asked her. At least this way, I would have a chance to talk to her, apologise, and Paul would never need to know.

"When do you need me to be here?"

"Seven."

"No problem. And she has the key and everything? You just need me to turn up?"

"Absolutely. Easy peasy."

"I guess then, I'll see you at about 9ish."

Karina excused herself, saying she had to get back to work. I bid her farewell, but all I could think about was whether Marie-Louise had forgiven me or not.

Chapter 17

For well over twelve hours my mind has been spinning around like a tumble dryer. I've been constantly churning around ideas about what possible reactions she might have when she sees me. I was apprehensive all night and unable to sleep. Now, at The Kennedys' street corner, I'm wondering if I should run away. Stupid I know – fully grown adult and I still have ideas about running away. But, I made a promise to Paul and I intend to keep it. That promise is the only thing stopping me from going home now.

Here at the front door, I can see no-one in either direction. It's nearly seven and Paul said she would be here, spot on. She doesn't strike me as the kind of girl that would be late, but when I think of it, I actually know next to nothing about her or her personal habits. Someone who appears to be an angel at work could still be the devil at home. There appears to be a light coming from under the office door. I guess, Paul left it on last night by mistake, he did have other things on his mind after all. I'll just mooch around for a minute or two and see if she turns up.

Granted, I do know little about her, but I am sure she would not be late for Paul. On the other hand, she might well be early. She has a key, she could be in the office. Maybe I should look inside. That's odd, the door is open. So much for the the quiet entrance! At any time she will come out of the office and her face will fall as she transforms the expectation of Paul, into the reality of Craig. I should wait for her to make the first move.

Still, she is a reasonable person. I am sure she will forgive me. It's possible she has already realised it's not Paul. Maybe he left a note for her in the office, in which case she will definitely not come out to greet me. At some point here I am just going to have to swallow my pride. Come on Craig, just walk in and apologise!

I open the door and feel confused. Sitting on the chair looking at me is what appears to be a person in dark clothes and a balaclava. I blink, I think he does the same. Yes, it clearly is a person in dark clothes wearing a balaclava. A split second passes and something comes at me from behind. All my senses go blunt. Someone jerks my hand behind my back, something cold is placed against my neck, words bounce against my ear drum, I am marched forward slowly. The sitting man stands up and turns to his side, so I can be guided past him. I see something behind his chair on the floor. It's Marie-Louise! What is happening? I am shoved down and my head meets the concrete floor, dislodging any thoughts that this might be a joke. He shouts something in my ear, but I don't hear it. Marie-Louise might be unconscious, or worse. I stare at her while my mind tries to work out what is going on. The man repeats his question.

"WHERE'S THE FUCKIN' KEY TO THE SAFE?"

"What" I respond. My nose, which was blocked, is now starting to run. The contents are about to fall on the floor, but I can't raise my arm in case they think I am starting something. I snort sharply to pull back the snot.

"NO NEED TO CRY KIDDO. JUST TELL US WHERE THE SAFE KEY IS AND WE'LL BE AWAY IN NO TIME."

I think it is unwise to set the record straight about not crying. Especially, since whatever he had against my neck, didn't feel friendly. Also, I'm shit scared and don't want to provoke them.

"I don't know, I don't work here, I am just a friend."

"TWO PEOPLE HERE ON A SATURDAY MORNING COME TO OPEN THE SHOP AND NEITHER OF YOU HAVE THE SAFE KEY. DO YOU THINK WE'RE FUCKIN' STUPID?"

"I don't work here, this is just a favour. The owner will be here later, that's why I'm here." I hope I am not dropping Paul in it here with my confession.

He yanks my arms behind my back again and I wriggle like a beached fish. I voluntarily put my hands together and he wraps something thin, tightly around them. I have been bending backwards to keep my head from lying on the ground, but the strain is overwhelming and I lay my head down on the cold ground. I am relieved to see Marie-Louise's back move up and down. At least she is breathing.

A sharp kick to the the ribs brings me back to reality, or fantasy, there is little to tell them apart. The men are mumbling something to one another, but my senses are not too sharp and I don't want them to think I am listening in. I focus on Marie-Louise. I pivot my head sideways along the floor and look at her prone body. Is she breathing, or is it just me breathing quicker?

How could this have happened? Surely she would not have been here too early, and I was outside barely five minutes. I'm sure I got to the door before seven. She could have been alone in here for well over ten minutes.

Why the hell did I agree to do this for Paul?

Get a grip now. I am OK and Marie-Louise appears to be. Does she have the key to the safe? I have no idea if she has it, or even needs it, or if it's something that only Paul deals with. If she has locked up on her own at night and been the last to leave the café, she must have needed the safe key before. She might well know where it is. If she does, I wish she would just tell them.

I am starting to feel very cold. So much for Hollywood heroism, I just want to see this through. They have been really quiet for the last few minutes. I think the office door is opening. If one of them has gone into the café there is only one in the office now. I want to look up, at least to see how big the one who grabbed hold of me is. Mind you, if they catch me looking I am sure I will cop another boot for my troubles.

I see Marie-Louise jerk a little. Maybe something is happening to her, but it could just be shock. She might be crying. I am starting to well up and my throat is as dry as sandpaper. God, what on earth am I doing here? The last few weeks I have just been coming back everyday to this café to see a girl who can't even stand me. I had a long term girlfriend who dumped me and I just grabbed at the first straw that came along. My job might be in jeopardy, if my boss finds out I have been well enough to come here every day. I have a shit job, few friends, no love life, no prospect of one. I have two months left on an apartment contract I can barely afford.

The swell in my eyes has blurred my vision and as I blink, a few tears drop down onto the floor. There is nothing like being a hostage to make one feel solipsistic!

I resolve right here, right now, if I get out of this, I will do something, *any*thing to change my life. I shouldn't be feeling like this: I have money; I have an education; I have friends; I have a job; and I also have no ties, no children, no mortgage. I need to sort this out while I still have control of my life.

What was that? I definitely heard a crash from the café. And another one. The door opens and somebody moves through it. I hold my breath for a few seconds and am sure there is no-one in the room. I swing my head round, foolishly, but am relieved to see no-one in the office. I turn to Marie-Louise.

"Are you OK?" Did she twitch? I can't hear anything. "Marie-Louise, are you OK?" Nothing. "It's all right, they have left the office. Just say yes if you can hear me."

"Yes." It was very quiet and tentative, but a definite yes. Trouble is, I am not sure if she was saying yes to let me know she can hear me, or yes she is all right.

"Are you OK?"

"Yes...where are they?"

"Not sure. Can't hear anymore in the..." The door opens and slams against the wall. One guy comes in and sees my head up. I don't think he heard me, but with my head raised and staring at him I notice the big guy behind him has his balaclava up. It's only a glimpse and I can only see black skin. The guy in front turns and pulls the balaclava down over the head of the other, swearing at him. When he turns back, we are staring eyeball to eyeball. Through the balaclava, I think I can make out white skin and bright blue eyes. He squints his eyes, plants one foot and buries the other one in my face.

Stars, salt, a stream of red, and then I go limp. I raise my head just in time to see him coming in again for my ribs. Oxygen is desperate to escape my body and for a second it feels like none will come back in. I breathe out a little more and then breathe in. The breath I draw, stops. I cannot draw in any more air. I breathe out, but when I breathe in again it stops. I feel overwhelmingly nauseated and vomit on the floor below my head. Weakness and relief combine with gravity and I drop my face into it.

"WHERE'S THE FUCKIN' KEY?"

I think it's a rhetorical question. It echoes in my head and is the last thing I hear before I black out.

Chapter 18

I had no idea how long I had passed out for. It felt like I had just fallen asleep for a second. I woke up with the previous nights puréed dinner making an island of my face. The last words I had heard buzzed around my brain. I had no idea if they were they still in the office. I slid my face towards Marie-Louise and was relieved to see her still there; not so relieved to realise what I had just slid my face on.

I could hear no sounds from the main café, although the throb in my head was all encompassing. What had happened? I couldn't quite process that someone had been in the room asking for the safe key, it seemed surreal. My arms were loosely bound behind my back and I remembered someone kicking me and telling me not to cry. Bursts of light orbited my head. I carelessly ignored the possible presence of others. I decided to roll over onto my back so I could relax my muscles a little. As I did so, I heard a quiet whimper from Marie-Louise and bullets of pain darted up my muscles towards my head. They all arrived at the same time and I thought I would black out again. The bullets embedded themselves in the back of my head and started to throb annoyingly like a student crowd having an unruly debate.

Although I wanted to fall unconscious, I was aware the door to the café was still unlocked and anyone could walk in. The irony of this already having happened was lost on me.

I sat up, sure that I looked like I was trying to scratch my back whilst in a straight jacket. Every jerk, painfully reminded me of my limitations. I hauled myself upright, but had to rest against a cupboard to regather some strength.

"Marie-Louise, are you all right?"

"Yes. Are they gone?"

"I think so. Are you hurt at all, did they hurt you?"

"No, they didn't really touch me except to throw me down." I could see she was shivering. I got up on my knees and tried to move across to her, but stopped halfway to rest on my bottom. She looked up a little and saw me slouched down, bleeding and stained with vomit. She quickly sat up.

"Oh my God, what did they do to you?" My appearance explained much better than I could. "Did they hit you?"

"Not much...not really...I can't really..." She seemed to notice my hands were tied and moved round behind me to undo them. There was a strange relief at having my hands free again, almost as if behind my body was their natural position. We looked at each other and then embraced, pulled by a magnet of relief. It was both comforting and painful. I never thought I would hug with her without sexual thoughts.

I was first to pull away, suddenly feeling self-conscious about my vomit, blood and smell. It was not the ideal first hug by any means. Her tears were still falling in a constant stream and I placed my hands either side of her face and used my thumbs to wipe them away. She was pallid.

"Are you sure you're OK?" I said.

She nodded in response. "Just...shocked."

"What did they do? Did they surprise you?"

"Yes, I was unlocking the door. They were walking the other way, but seemed to be in conversation, laughing and joking. Then when I pushed the door open they were following me in from behind."

"So you saw them on the street! Were they wearing balaclavas?" Another jolt of pain peaked in my head making me dizzy, and I missed the start of her answer.

"...why do you ask?"

I steadied myself with my hands on the floor.

"When I got here, they were wearing balaclavas. I guess it would have been a bit suspicious if they walked along the street with them on. Do you remember what they looked like?"

"Not really. They seemed deep in conversation and I didn't really pay attention. One was white and one was black." Suddenly, I heard a feint sound from the café. It sounded like something being moved, rather than dropped. My pain it seemed, had gone away, or at least hidden itself, and I was enveloped by some unusual courage. I stood up using the desk as a prop and was surprised at how little pain I felt. I started walking towards the door of the office.

"What are you *doing*?"

I didn't answer her. I was looking for something to put in my hands. If someone was going to have another go at me, or us, I was going to be ready this time. In the corner, next to the door, was a broom. I reached out in slow motion and then placed my hand on the door, pausing for a second.

"Craig, what are you doing? Don't go out there!"

I pushed the handle down as quietly as possible and started to open the door. It seemed miked up to an amplifier and turned to full volume. Why is it, you never notice doors squeak until you have to open one quietly? As I peered through the crack in the door, I saw a cat prowling on one of the tables. I opened the door wider, expecting the cat to be the room's lone occupant, and moved out into the café standing between the toilet and office door, Marie-Louise clutching my jacket from behind.

The door to the café was open, and one of the guys with a balaclava was kneeling, collecting scattered beads off the floor. He looked up, putting the collected beads in his pocket as he got up to approach me. I noticed how much taller and beefier he was than me. He must have been the one who first grabbed me from behind. I raised my broom handle behind my head like a baseball player readying to take a swing. He paused. Saturday morning stood still, waiting to see what we would do. He turned and ran out the door, crushing some left-behind beads on his way.

A sharp pain shot up from my ribs. I dropped the broom and blacked out again.

Chapter 19

I came to, with Marie-Louise crouched over me. She was rocking me gently and had a phone in one hand.

"Craig, wake up. I have phoned the police. They should be here in a minute."

I was barely awake and managed a 'mmwwlll'.

"Craig, are you all right? Should I call an ambulance?" The last word roused me.

"No I'm OK. Did he come back?"

"No. I have locked the door anyway."

"Good idea." I closed my eyes and rested my head back on the ground.

"Should I call an ambulance? Your face is awfully red and swollen. What are you doing here? Where is Paul, he should be here by now?"

Her words drifted through my head, nothing sticking. One hour before, I was paranoid whether Marie-Louise was going to talk to me again. The feeling bobbed back up in my head. At least that problem was over. I registered her last question.

"He couldn't make it. He asked me to cover for him."

"Where is he? Why couldn't he make it?"

"He had to look after his kid last night and couldn't leave him early. He should be here about nine."

"It's nearly eight. Should I call him?"

"He'll soon be on his way by now. If the police are here soon, they will contact him themselves."

"So...you are here because he asked you to cover."

"Yeah. It might seem strange given what just happened, but I want to apologise for the other day. I said some really bad things to you, and I should have minded my own business."

"Craig, I'm sorry. What you said made sense, it just hurt to hear it, that's all. But you were only saying what you felt. I think I just felt guilty because I knew that I should have given my boyfriend a chance."

I felt dizzy and was afraid of opening my eyes and flooding my head with light.

"Yeah, but I knew nothing of the situation and was speaking without knowing all the facts."

"Nevertheless, you were quite right. I was just jealous. You wait here, I will get a cloth."

"A cloth?"

"Yes, you're bleeding from your face and...I want to clean it up."

"Oh, you mean the vomit. I must look a state. Sorry about the smell."

"Craig, don't worry. I nearly peed my pants, I was so scared. It sounds bad, but I was actually relieved when I heard you were in there with me. I didn't feel quite so...exposed."

"Not that I was much good."

"I don't think either of us had much chance."

"Did they get away with anything?"

"I didn't even look yet. My God, I should check everything!"

"No wait! Wait till the police come. They will want to check the place out, and take fingerprints."

I opened my eyes and saw her looking around feverishly, as if she had lost something. She felt her body, got up and looked around the café.

"What is it? What have you lost?"

"My purse. My bag. I had it over my shoulder when I came in. I must have dropped it when they took me in the office." She ran towards the office, opened the door and disappeared inside. I struggled to raise myself to my knees. As I was just getting myself up with the help of the table, she came out again. She had lost speed and purpose and started crying.

"They took my purse. It had everything in." She kept walking to me and dropped into my arms. I jumped as if a cat had jumped on my lap, digging its claws in. Pins prodded me all over my body. I let her cry for a minute, but she didn't seem to get any better. I pushed her back to arms length, looked into her eyes, and she began to cry harder. I could think of nothing to say and was beginning to feel nauseated. I decided it would be better to just keep hugging, even though I was unsure how much longer I would be able to support our weight whilst sitting upright. We sat there, staining the floor with blood and tears.

I don't know how long we were sitting, but that is how the police found us when they arrived. I heard a double tap on the window and was relieved to see them looking in: a policeman and a policewoman.

The man looked reassuringly big and muscular, and the woman compassionate. I released myself from Marie-Louise and went and opened the door. They immediately asked if we were all right and alone, and I suddenly felt the comfort of safety again.

The next half hour was spent explaining what had happened as best as we could recall. We were both certain that neither of us would be able to place a positive ID on them, if we were to see them again. I felt overwhelmed and helpless, and the questions made me more and more irritable. It was at this point that Paul arrived. He knocked on the door, even though it was his café and the door was open, but I guess it was to avoid startling anyone.

"What the hell happened?"

"Sir, there was an attempted robbery here this morning and this is a crime scene, may I ask you to step back outside, please." The policeman was firm, but not unfriendly.

"But this is my café. I am the owner. What do you mean a robbery?"

"Are you Paul Williams?"

"Yes, that's me."

"We have been trying to contact you, but without answer. We tried you at home and your mobile number."

"I was looking after my boy. I had to drop him off at his mother's. What happened?"

"Paul, I am so sorry. They jumped me when I came this morning. They followed me through the door and wanted the key to the safe."

"My God, are you OK?" I don't know what it is about shocking situations that make people lose all depth of vocabulary and sentence construction. Hollywood may employ poetic and heroic speeches in times of crisis, but these are far from realistic.

"Yes, I am now. Craig came so I wasn't alone. They didn't get away with anything."

"Except your purse." I felt the need to point this out again, as the policemen seemed less concerned when she mentioned this to them before.

"Where are they, have you caught them?" Paul said.

"No, sir. Miss Delhaise called after they had left and we arrived here a short while later." I did not initially realise they were talking about Marie-Louise. "Since then, we have been asking them questions, trying to establish what happened and also documenting the place. May I ask you a few questions now?"

"Uh, sure. So let me get this straight. You guys were jumped and then they tried to open the safe. Did they get away with anything?"

"It appears at the moment, that they got away with nothing. However, it would be helpful if you could verify that. It's possible your employees have missed something."

"Oh, actually I am not an employee." It seemed important to me to point that out.

"You're not? So what were you doing here?"

"Well, I am a regular here." I felt embarrassed. It seemed a rather irrelevant thing to say to a policeman, almost as if I was bragging about it.

"You're a regular? A little early to be turning up for coffee, isn't it?"

"No, Paul asked me to. He said last night that he was unable to come in this morning and could I cover for him."

"Is this true?" The policeman sought confirmation from Paul in a rather accusatory manner.

"Yes, that's right. I got an emergency call from my ex. She asked if I could look after our boy last night and I thought it would be too much for him to bring him here early this morning. Instead, I asked Craig if he could cover for me."

"We should continue our interview somewhere else, sir. Another unit will be along in a minute to help. May I ask, how many people work here in total?"

"Just me, Marie-Louise, and another guy Thomas."

"And do you all have access to the office?"

"Yes, they are free to go in there when they need to."

"And why might they need to?"

"I can't help but feel like I have done something wrong here officer."

The policeman seemed to ignore this objection.

"Do you all have keys to the safe?"

"Yes, they have access. They need it when they lock up."

"We just need to know how many people use the office. If there are many people coming and going, then there is little point dusting for prints. It seems pointless dusting this part of the café and behind the counter similarly so. They didn't exactly stop for coffee."

Paul noticed the smashed cups on the floor, and various other bits of crockery scattered between them. His shoulders dropped a little as it visibly hit him that his own café had been violated.

Paul led the policeman into the office and his partner stayed in the main café with us.

"Can I make you two a drink of something? Something warm might be good for you."

Marie-Louise nodded, and got up to help her with sweeping up and making hot chocolates. The policewoman said that caffeine would not be good for us as we were still in shock. As Marie-Louise brought the drinks over, the policewoman helped me up on to a chair. My face had started to feel like it was expanding and I felt very self-conscious as to how I looked. Another two police officers arrived. They discussed things with their colleague, and Marie-Louise and I were left alone again.

As the hot chocolate came close to my mouth, the steam off it jabbed at the injuries on my face and it reminded me of the kick I received there.

Paul came out out of the office, sat down with us and the three of us sat in silence. I was vaguely aware the police officers were documenting things and taking notes. Words seemed pointless. Every predictable question one of us might ask, had a predictable answer. Paul stood again and started clearing up. Marie-Louise offered to help him, but he was very forceful in refusing her help, saying she should rest.

The officers had a few more questions and then Paul ordered taxis for us. He wanted us both to go to the hospital, but Marie-Louise point blank refused, insisting she went home. As he put her in the taxi, he said he would ring her tomorrow, but she should take the week off work. I tried to refuse to go to the hospital as well, but my face seemed to join in the argument against me and I gave in. One of the policewomen said she would come with me and got in the taxi. As we drove away from the café I could see Jam Man walking up to the door with a plastic bag in his hand, no doubt holding his precious latest jam. It was the first everyday thing to happen to me that day. The first extraordinary thing still awaited him.

Chapter 20

At the hospital, I was finally able to see myself in the mirror, and winced in pity for Marie-Louise hugging me – and, when I saw myself they had cleaned up the vomit from my face! After giving me a couple of stitches above my left eye, they allowed me to go home. It had started bleeding again in the hospital and I just went with whatever recommendation they offered. They said I had mild concussion and asked if there was someone at home to look after me. I lied. They also saw to my hand, which had started to turn a very dark purple, and wrapped it up in a bandage. I went home and spent the rest of the day and night in bed. I drifted in and out of sleep, and kept replaying events over and over. I ate nothing and my sole intake was tea.

After a disturbed Sunday spent at home in further contemplation, and despite feeling mentally and physically fragile, the café seemed the only place to go on Monday. I wasn't even sure if it would be open, but it seemed the only place where people might understand what had happened. It was an experience I could not put into words. Others could imagine it, but unless they were there, cannot truly understand it. I had to see Marie-Louise because I needed to talk about what had happened without being asked all the juicy details. The inside of my skull felt bruised from throwing thoughts around.

I walked in and instantly felt like I had just completed a jigsaw puzzle. It's amazing how one experience can change the way you view a place, and the place looked completely different to me now. Having previously only seen the café as a customer, Saturday morning had reversed my view to that of an employee and I had become fully acclimated.

I was disappointed that Marie-Louise was not there. Only then did I remember Paul's last words to her on Saturday, offering her the week off. How could I forget that. I still hoped she might come in and want to talk to me or Paul.

Paul was there and Thomas was back. Paul couldn't hold the shock in when he saw my hand, face and the stitches. His greeting was garnished with clear concern.

"Oh well, can't complain."

"Well, you could, but nobody's listening." Such a weak offering was most unlike Paul. I got the feeling he felt guilty about what had happened, even though he had no reason to.

"And how are you? Have you managed to sort everything out with the café?"

"Well, I spent most of yesterday clearing up the place. Insurance company is being a pain. They said it's not so clear cut because the robbers didn't force entry and said they would have to send someone out to look over the place, and wait for the police report. Hopefully, it's just them being funny on the phone. I can't see with all the police records and stuff how they can deny it."

"Have you spoken to Marie-Louise?" I was keen to extend my altruism.

"Yeah, I spoke to her last night. She's still a bit shaken up. I told her to take the week off, but she said she would be all right to work. We compromised – she's coming back tomorrow."

I felt lost without her. It was as though I was sixteen again and had gone to the house of my girlfriend, who wasn't there, and was left twiddling my thumbs in front of her dad.

"Let me get you a coffee. Take a seat, I'll bring it over."

I sat down next to the window. Jam Man was at the next table, the only familiar face. I couldn't raise a smile.

"Mmwwm...hello." As he spoke, bits of apple muffin flew out onto the table. "Mmmwmmm...sorry." He wiped them away. "Heard what happened. Awful, awful."

"Pardon." He still had a little ball of muffin attached to the crack of his mouth. I couldn't focus on anything else.

"The robbery. Paul told me what happened. It's an awful business."

I had never noticed how old Jam Man looked before. Being closer to him and in the light, the wrinkles seemed highlighted for my benefit.

"Huh. Oh yeah. It could have been worse."

"Well, thank you for saving the place! Don't know what I'd do without it. Only place that lets me get my jam out on the table."

Any other day the double entendre of this line would have had me in stitches. Today it didn't seem so funny.

"I tried in a few other places...", he seemed unperturbed by my disinterest; "...but they only tolerated it for a few days and then asked me to put it away." I smiled politely and he continued like a comic plugging away at an unresponsive audience. "One place asked me immediately if I wouldn't mind 'putting my jam away'. I mean, what kind of question is that? You can't get your jam out in here they said. Everyone will see it." It was becoming harder and harder to stay serious in this bombardment of ludicrousness. "Everybody else is satisfied with my muffins they said! Why do you have to jam my muffins they said! Paul has never had a problem with my jam. And he does the best apple muffins. Never gives me a hard time. Hard to find that in a place these days. I mean, what is the world coming to when I can't sit in a café and jam my muffins in piece."

I could hold it no more. I burst out laughing. I meant no disrespect to the guy, but it was impossible not to laugh when met with someone so passionate about putting jam on muffins. Three weeks previous, I would have written him off as an intruder of my space. A freak. Someone to be ignored and moaned about. Yet here, it seemed plainly obvious to me, he was just reaching out. He may not have had the normal conversational topics, but he was genuine, and right then and there, I needed someone genuine.

"You always use the same jam?"

"For sure, I make my own. Many, many different varieties." My mind started to compile a list as to what they might be, but given my limited brain capacity at that moment I couldn't get past strawberry and raspberry."

"So which one do you like most?" He got up, plate of jammed muffin in one hand, coffee in the other and took one step towards me. He paused as if realising he was doing something that someone has expressly told him not to. I sensed he was lonely.

"Would it be all right to join you, or do you want to be alone?"

"No come on over. I'm on my own."

I cringed at this picture. My life had come to sharing tables in cafés with jam enthusiasts. It was not a picture I wanted to encourage. He placed his plate on my table, one bite left on one muffin, the other one waiting to be smeared. He laid the milky coffee down next to it.

"Well, I like apple muffins. I don't always have apple muffins, but all the other flavours are too imposing in flavour and you need a complementary taste, not an opposing one. Subtlety: that's the key to a good muffin!" It sounded like it was going to be a lecture on baking. "As for what goes best with apple, I tried many types, but you need something that is not overpowering or too sweet. For me, raspberry goes best with apple. Blueberry also goes well. I have tried many combinations, at least fifteen."

"You've tried fifteen jams with apple muffins?" I entertained the possibility that he might be a jam salesman.

"No, that would be ridiculous. I have tried them with other things. I have only tried apple muffins with eight jams, but I keep coming back to blueberry or raspberry."

"And your favourite flavour overall?"

"Jam or muffin?"

"Jam."

"Raspberry and Pomegranate. No question. But not with muffins. And it's not easy to get good pomegranates, not to mention the expense."

"That sounds an interesting...combination." I feared that we would soon exhaust the possibilities to talk about jam and be left with little else. Luckily, Paul came over with my coffee.

"How's the jam, Stan?"

I found it hilarious that his name was Stan. Stan the Jam Man!

"Wonderful, you want some Paul?" I could think of very little, less appealing than being offered a jammed muffin from a man with some stuck to the corner of his moustache, and aged stains on his jacket. I wanted to see how Paul would get out of this one.

"Oh, go on then." He took the remaining bite on the plate. "Mmm, blueberry, the best with that muffin." I must have been staring at Paul in disbelief.

"Would you like some, Craig?" I realised that if I were to turn Stan down now, it would seem rude. Various excuses crossed my mind, but none connected with my voice. Fortunately, his second muffin lay untouched.

"Oh go on, what the hell!"

This seemed to please Stan no end. With a big grin on his face, he cut a piece off and got the jam from his bag, handling it like a precious gem. He was fully concentrating on the task in hand, as I was on him and Paul on me – a pure chain of concentration. When he had finished, he handed it to me with such expectation on his face, I realised it was an important moment. I treated the moment with the respect it deserved, placed the muffin piece in my mouth and savoured the initial taste. Then I started to chew and as the flavour spread. It was indeed, a great combination.

"That's pretty fucking good."

Stan looked very happy that his delicacy had got the thumbs up.

"This calls for more muffins" said Paul. He promptly went off and came back with a plate of six muffins. "I was going to throw them. They are from Saturday so not too fresh, but the jam will moisten them up."

Stan's eyes lit up. What better did I have to do?

The next hour we spent eating apple muffins and trying different jams. It turned out that Stan had four other varieties in his bag and we promised to reimburse him as we ploughed our way through them. We chopped and changed muffins with jams, each time urging others to try new combinations we found exciting. I bought some more drinks and had the longest discussion on jam I had ever had. I was pleasantly surprised to find Stan so garrulous. I gradually felt a weight ease from my shoulders.

My fun was shattered shortly after Stan had left. I had decided to stay in the café for a while longer, when my pocket started vibrating. I had the not irregular feeling I shouldn't answer the phone, but something compelled me to do so. As I answered it, a familiar voice cut mine off.

"Craig spea..."

"Hello Craig. Where are you exactly?" It was my boss. I contemplated lying but his directness belied a warm, 'just out of interest' tone. A tone which hints at the speaker knowing more than they are letting on.

"Um, at the moment, I have just gone for a little walk." I left a short gap and he gave no indication of filling it. "I'm in a café."

"Oh, what café would that be exactly?" My mind started whirling with all the possibilities involved. In one of them, he was spying on me and I instinctively looked out the window for him, on the street, then behind bins and wall-corners.

"It's one in Camden actually. I had to give something back to someone. They lent me something and it was urgent." Please don't ask me what it is. Please don't ask me what it is.

"What is it?"

"Um, a um, a, some money. They had lent me some money."

"Would this be the café round the corner from work?"

"Well, it's not that far away granted, but..."

"Can I suggest that you pop into work then on the way back, if that's not too much trouble."

The words were polite, but he was smearing his speech with heavy dollops of sarcasm.

"Well, I was just going to go home actually, I feel a little exhausted." There was another pause. It was high noon, both of us waiting for the other to twitch. I might have cracked had I had a strong urge towards protecting my job, or placating him, but I was empty. I felt nothing.

"All right then, we can talk on the phone. One of my employees – your colleague, although you would not know her yet as you have not been here in such a long time – told me that she met you in a café. She suggested you were very happy, talkative, sociable and showed none of the usual signs of one suffering from depression. I was wondering what you had to say about this." I was ill-prepared for such a conversation. He knew something about my recent life, but I had no idea how much.

"Well, I have good and bad days. I mean, I am nearly back on track, although it has been very difficult."

"Yes, I am sure. I saw your *ex*-girlfriend last week. She came into here wanting to speak to you. She said she wanted to meet up with you and knew you would ignore her phone calls. She was surprised to hear you were off work with depression. Seems you had not told her." I didn't know what to be angrier about: his emphasis on the word ex or that he told her about my depression. I remembered how surprised she seemed when I told her in the café. I guess, she was nice enough to not bring it up in fear of embarrassing me.

"I actually wanted to keep that secret. Or not so much a secret, but I did not want her to know."

"Oh, I'm sorry. I didn't think of that." Yeah right! "Your new colleague, the one you have been socialising with in the café, also said you were working."

"Working! I don't know where she got that idea from."

"So you weren't working on Saturday? At the café. The Kennedys. A couple of hundred metres from here. While you were on sick leave from your real job." He left a little pause to let the panic set in. "Because if you were doing that, I'm sure you're aware that would be illegal."

"Hang on! Are you just believing her over me? She could say anything. I wasn't working Saturday. I was just helping out a friend."

"The help: was it in the form of work?"

"No, he just wanted me to look after one of his employees."

"What are they, a pet?"

"No, a woman."

"Look after, as in a supervisory role?"

"No, it was for her protection. It was early in the morning and the manager was unable to be here, so I helped open up the shop."

"*Open up the shop?*" I started to resent his onslaught and the anger was swelling up in me. "Is that not a supervisory role?"

"Supervisory role! I actually turned up to make sure that nothing bad happened. As a result of which, I was jumped, held hostage, beaten up and kept face down in an office with a knife, or gun, I have no idea which. Therefore, I ache, am physically and mentally shaken and yes I am sitting in a café, as I have done most days, to relax and get over the fact that Kate ripped my heart out and I'm learning to survive without one. The last place I want to be is work and your sarcastic digs make that desire even less, so sorry if I am drinking coffee on the company's time, but that's just the way it is."

I felt triumphant. I had told him in no uncertain terms how I felt, answered all his unanswered questions and justified my actions. He had no possible come back to me.

"Craig, your doctor's certificate was for three weeks. I feel you have breached the parameters of your sick leave, but I am willing to let that slide. I will put it simply: either you come back to work next Monday when your leave ends, or don't come back at all. Is that clear?"

Nausea swept over my body like a rising tide. I felt short of air.

"Yes, very clear."

"OK, see you at nine on Monday."

He hung up. It was just as well he did this as I was on the verge of pointing out that one of the options he gave me would involve me not seeing him on Monday. Now I just had to decide which option to take.

Chapter 21

I stormed out after the phone call had ended. I started off in the direction of the shop, but gut instinct talked me out of it. Fortunately, a passing bus was there to whisk me home before I did something I would regret.

I felt as if everything had been stripped away from me like having my legs waxed. I had quickly been relieved of: my girlfriend; my job security; and my own safety, which I had previously taken for granted. True, it was longer than the one second peeling away of wax, but when the previous four weeks are placed in the context of a lifetime, the feeling left me just as shocked. I got home, brooded for an hour and then decided I simply had to talk to someone, someone who at least knew some of the recent mess: I rang Kim. I am not the best person at bearing my soul to others. In fact, vulnerability is something I generally avoid like scaffolding in the street. I left a message on his answer phone suggesting we hook up – I was free any time this week and chances were I would be hanging around the café. I realised in a rather dejected moment, how much the café had become my crux.

Kim didn't phone back until the Tuesday morning by which time, I had calmed down a little. I was on the bus on the way to Camden.

"Sorry Craig, I've been so bogged down in studies at the moment, I'd completely forgotten to phone you. How are you? What have you been up to?"

"I've started drinking sugar in my coffee. It's a big step for me."

"Any particular reason?" Kim asked.

"I hate sugar in coffee."

"Why are you drinking it then?"

"A little enforced discomfort has been liberating. OK, liberating is hardly the world, but I'm learning to become less rigid."

"Well, that sounds good...I think. Anything else?"

"Not really. I got my hand trapped in a door and I told Kate that I wanted her back."

"That couldn't have been easy. What did she say?"

"That she has started seeing that other guy and is moving in with him."

"Seriously, what did she say?"

"That really is what she said." Kim did not answer me immediately, and rather than dwell on that point I pushed the conversation onwards. Given what I wanted to say, I had a feeling akin to standing at the top of a ski slope for the first time. Whether I was going to cry or not was completely arbitrary. "I have helped out a bit at the café, with a delivery and serving coffee. Shouted at Marie-Louise and told her she had treated her boyfriend like shit. Got held hostage in an armed robbery. I met a new colleague from work and they have found out I spend every day in The Kennedys. She told my manager she saw me here and when he phoned me to ask about it, I shouted at him. He gave me an ultimatum: come to work next Monday or I am out. I guess he will say that I have been not acting in accordance with someone who is off work with depression. Oh, and I have become quite partial to apple muffins with jam."

Up to then, I had shown no signs of falling off my skis and was actually starting to feel like confessing things was a hobby I could make a go of. Kim took up the role of father.

"Seems like you have been keeping quite busy. What the hell do you have planned next?"

"I think I might try milk in my coffee."

We talked for a little more and I filled him in with some details. He explained that he had his final oral exam the next day and had been studying furiously for that. He also had his placement interview for Mali the following Monday and so had been preparing for that as well. He agreed to meet up in the café Friday lunchtime.

I finished the conversation, got off the bus and took the short walk to The Kennedys. A surprising calm consumed me, but when I got there, I was once again disappointed by her absence and when Paul told me she was not coming in, I became desperate.

"What do you mean she is having another day off?" My frustration seemed inverse to Paul's patience.

"She isn't doing too well, Craig. I phoned her last night to offer her the week off again and she said she would take just another day. Sounds like you could do with a break yourself."

"Last thing I need is another person telling me what to do."

"Whoa, hold on! I was just concerned that's all. And as for Marie-Louise, she's not having much luck on the domestic front either."

"What does *that* mean?"

"She had a big fight with her boyfriend, or ex-boyfriend, I don't know. Whatever he is at the moment, they had a big row."

"Did she say what about? Surely he should be going easy on her at the moment."

"You're one to talk! Besides, it is not my business to ask questions as to what might be the matter. I offered her time off and she has taken it, albeit a day. You seem like you are on a bit of a short fuse yourself at the moment."

I had been so proud of how calmly I had recounted my recent life events to Kim without cracking. I had finished my ski slope without wavering. Now however, I had transferred my journey to a boat, and after a sudden blow to my port side, I was taking on water.

"I'm just fucked off with everything." I took a look round the café to see who my audience was. Donna was there with Matt, and the Professor was alone at the back of the café, making himself comfortable for my coming performance. Other than that, the faces were all new to me. I nodded in the direction of Matt, who reciprocated in kind. The leak had been plugged for a while and I didn't want another scene.

"That's a pretty big thing to be fucked off with. You seemed all right yesterday. Something happen last night?"

"Actually, it happened just after Stan left and you cleared the table. I got a phone call."

"Come to think of it, I don't remember you leaving. We had a bit of a rush on as I recall."

"My boss called me."

"What's the problem?"

"He gave me an ultimatum. Either I go back to work on Monday, or I don't come back at all."

He looked right through me, as if I had disappeared.

"What exactly is the problem there?"

"He's just so fucking unreasonable."

"I think most managers would expect that kind of commitment out of their employees. I don't think he is different to anyone else."

"But my life is just so up in the air at the moment. I have no idea what I'm doing, how I'm feeling about anything. I'm still trying to get over Kate. I just don't want to go back to work."

"Then don't."

The way he said it was so simple! It didn't sound like a rash threat or trying to prove a long forgotten point: it was the right thing to do, because that was what I wanted to do. But every part of me was telling myself it was the wrong thing to do.

All I could think about was what people would think. It would feed my father's disappointment in me: his idea of work was to go for your first day at 16, then spend 50 years working for the same firm, accept a modest pension, live a few years and die. The firm is not there for us, we are there for them.

My mother would roll her eyes and then tell her friends over tea: "it's just Craig trying to prove a point. I'm surprised he stayed so long in this job to tell the truth."

My work colleagues would all congratulate me. Pat me on the back in fake admiration, telling me I was the lucky one for having escaped. Then, when they found out I had nothing else to go to, they would adjust their voices trying to hide their surprise, ask me if I was joking, and walk away in a it's-your-life superior strut.

Apart from Kim, most of my friends are halfway up career ladders of their own. Too far up to see the bottom, but no nearer to the top than they ever were. The thought of leaving a job because you didn't like it would never enter their heads, unless they had another job signed, sealed and delivered already – naturally on the next rung up.

And for some reason, these were the only people I thought of when I wondered what people would think. I always seem to view the other people, like Kim, Paul, Marie-Louise and Bobby K, as a little bit strange. They had never really done it the way we learned at school. Sure, you can drift a little after school, but sooner or later your journey finds the tracks and then you just ride the train till you die. I never had the courage to do what they do. They seem so temporary, and I find permanence too comforting.

Imaginary conversation at school with your Careers Advisory Officer:

"So, what would you like to be when you grow up?"

"Nothing. I want to have a simple job, earn enough to get by, and enjoy my life outside of work."

"But what about ambition, what about achievement, what about money?"

"My ambition is to have a nice family and be happy."

"What kind of ambition is that?!?"

"I actually want to put that under the achievement box – 'is happy.'"

"Nice dream, but you can't put 'happy' and 'family' under the financial security box."

"I said I wanted enough to get by. I wouldn't have a family if I had no money, but I don't want to have money and hate everything else about my life."

"I'm sorry to tell you son, that's just not how it's done."

It was then it struck me that the doctor was right: I was depressed. I was in a situation where I had all the money I needed, and I was not happy. I hated everything else. I leave work and go home to an empty void. I had believed that Kate and I were totally happy and in reality she was right: we were a mess. I thought she made me happy, but instead she allowed me to avoid focusing on the lack of everything else in my life. That was what my life had become: a lack.

Trouble is, when you realise you are approaching thirty and live in a lack, how do you change? Surely it was too late? The thought of doing a simple job at my age would seem somewhat like I was underachieving. I had been to university and serving coffee or wiping people's drool was not something that would be utilising my qualifications.

"It's not that simple Paul. I can't just serve coffee for the rest of my life, can I?"

"That's my plan."

"Yeah, but you must have something else figured."

"Nope."

"Mind you, you are a business owner. You don't just serve coffee."

"Lou 'just serves coffee'. Thomas has two jobs – he also works in a pub round the corner. Do you think there is something wrong with doing that as a job?"

"No, it's fine on a temporary basis. But what do want to say to your little boy: when you grow up you can serve coffee just like me?"

"What's wrong with that?"

"It's a bit of an...well, an underachievement."

"Based on what?"

"You are an educated man. You could do so much. Don't you find serving people all day a little...degrading?" Try as I might, the pause hadn't helped me find a better word to use.

"Craig, it may have escaped your attention, but in the last month you have spent most days in this café. If I didn't 'degrade myself', where would you have gone? You were certainly happy enough to have found us here."

Two old ladies who had been supping cappuccinos at the back of the café, got up and wished Paul a lovely day by name, and he reciprocated with surnames. The community here was pretty much down to Paul. Sure, he had the help of a few other people, but he was always the constant. And it had been the source of all my happiness in the previous three weeks.

"Your right. I am sorry. I think it's great if you can do that. For me though, I can't just give up everything and take a step back to serving coffee. I wish I could, but I can't."

"What do you mean 'give up everything' and 'take a step back' to serving coffee? What is so great about the everything you have at the moment? You said yourself how unhappy you are in your job. And why is going from selling electrical products to serving coffee a step back? Don't you just bleed people dry of their money as a salesman anyway? Seems to me there is something a whole lot more ethical about serving coffee if that's the case."

"I know, I know. Like I said, I wish I could do what you do, but I can't. I admire you."

"It may have escaped your attention, but the girl you seem to have your eye on in this café also 'just serves coffee'. I bet you don't think anything less of her." I was so engrossed in defending my position I scarcely registered his observation about my feelings for her.

"No, but I am sure she will not be doing that in ten years time."

"Why?"

"Because it's not a career that's why!"

"And what exactly is a career?"

There was anger in his voice. An answer eluded me. It was such a simple question and one I was completely unable to give a satisfactory answer to.

"Well, it's a...you get the chance...if you want...you can move up...higher. If you want to, you can move up higher. To a better job. And improve yourself."

"And that's what you want is it? You are in a career job now – What is the next step up?"

"Well, I don't want to move up, but if I did it would be manager. Or at least assistant and then manager."

"So if you don't want it, what's the big deal with being in that system? You said you're not happy doing that. Why does it matter if you stay at the same level selling TVs or selling coffee?"

"But what would people think of me?"

"There comes a time in everybody's life when you just have to say fuck it. Do what you want, think what you want. As for what everyone else thinks about you, fuck it! The ones that are genuine people will support you; the others are just thinking about themselves, not you. Maybe they give you a hard time because they are jealous that you have the courage to do what they want to do. Isn't that kind of the way you feel anyway?"

I felt a liquid slowly flooding my eyeballs. A strange grip had taken hold of my heart, squeezing it gently. My heart rate increased and grasshoppers began jumping in my stomach. I had no idea why I felt so nervous, but just thinking about the possibilities made me terrified and excited.

Thomas came in. Paul continued to look at me, whilst wiping his hands and backing away. He talked to Thomas, who was carrying a plastic bag full of things for the café. Paul went back into the office with Thomas's coat, and Thomas started unpacking the things.

"You want a drink?"

"No thanks. I'm heading off in a minute."

He nodded in acceptance. In the time that I had spent with Thomas, he had never spoken more than a smattering of words to anyone.

"How long have you been in England, Thomas?"

"Nearly two years now."

"Why did you come, if you don't mind my asking?"

"To get money for my family."

"Your family came with you?"

"No, my brother studies here at the moment, but my wife and children are in Angola."

"When did you last go back home?"

"I have not been back since I came here."

"How old are your children?"

"Five and seven."

"Don't you miss them?"

"Yes, but there is war in Angola. It is not safe and I have no chance to make enough money for my family."

"So you send the money back to them."

"Yes, this is true."

"How long do you want to stay here?"

"I don't want to stay, but if I go back, my family will starve because I have no money, or I will have to fight. You don't want coffee?"

I shook my head. There was little I could say. I thought about all the options I had that Thomas didn't. I cringed when I imagined what Thomas's reaction might be if I told him about my problems as I had just told Paul. I made a shameful exit.

Chapter 22

Walking into the café the next day, my heart thawed. She looked up from making a cappuccino and smiled in my direction. Her smile quickly melted away as she timidly offered the drink to the customer and took the money. She looked smaller somehow, fragile, no longer the beguiling girl who bounded through the door nearly three weeks before.

"How are you?" I said.

"Fine, thanks. You?"

"I've been better. Can I buy you a drink?"

"Thank you no, I have one. I should be ready for a break in a minute. Do you want to sit down? I can join you." My cheeks turned apricot red with her offer.

"Any preference of table?" I looked around and realised there was only one table free. "Window seat?"

"I'll be there in a minute."

She prepared a coffee, washed her hands, and shyly knocked on the office door. She popped her head in and then came back, took her apron off and collected the coffee. She took a seat, pushed the coffee under my slouching frame and cradled her orange juice.

"I'll just grab some sugar."

"You always drink black coffee. Anything else kills the taste, no?"

"Actually, I've started having sugar now."

"I understand. I love the smell of coffee and Paul has tried me with it, but I need a little syrup and milk in mine, otherwise it's too bitter."

"There are many people like that. Kate was like that. Give her any latte as long as it was flavoured and she would be happy." I was not comfortable mentioning her to Marie-Louise, but they had met so it was stupid to avoid it.

"That must have been annoying, with you being so passionate about coffee."

"Actually, no. I liked the fact that she had her own drink. It made her feel less of a puppet in my eyes. And I guess it gave me something to take the piss out of her for."

"Take the piss?"

"When I felt bad about myself, I felt superior to her by highlighting her poor choice of coffee in a conversation. It doesn't sound very nice does it?"

"Er, not really."

"It's fine, you can say it. I guess people do shitty things all the time, I know I certainly do. Truth is, we never really talked through anything. We just jumped to the arguing part. Even when we disagreed with each other in the past, we just ignored the other person when we had a problem. After a while we got bored of the silence and at some point started shouting instead."

An embarrassed smile came over her face.

"Me too. After we spoke the other day, I realised I was never happy with René's independence. I think I tried to overcompensate by controlling him. I didn't make life very easy for him."

"Have you seen him since Saturday?"

"Yes. But I wish I hadn't."

"Why?"

"It seems the women I accused him of sleeping with, the landlady; she actually tried something on him."

"He slept with her!"

"That's what I thought. I jumped to conclusions again when he told me. It seems nothing happened, but it highlighted to me that I don't trust him, or can't trust him, I don't know. Since Saturday, my emotions have been up and down from minute to minute; I wasn't fair to him."

Ordinarily, I would have tried to make her feel better or state that he had not been such a great guy. Instead, I needed to vent some of my own anger instead of bottling it up inside.

"I've not felt right since Saturday." I said. "I had a shit couple of days and the only person I wanted to speak to was you. I thought you would be the only person who would understand what I was feeling."

"I'm glad it wasn't just me. My friends wanted me to talk about it, but each time it felt like opening up a very private part of me and letting them in. And it felt like they would have no respect for that memory. No real idea how it felt to experience that."

"So have you come to any conclusions?"

"Actually, I have been thinking about stuff."

"You want to talk about it?"

"I've been thinking about going home for a while."

"Like a holiday." No response. "Good idea! Get away from things, clear your mind. How long for?"

"Not sure. I will see how I feel. It certainly shook my feeling of well-being and I realised I don't see or speak to my family enough and that bothers me."

I started to think about my situation. The last time I had spoken to my mum was four months ago. Contact with her was limited to Christmas and birthdays; it was nearer two years since I had seen her. I hadn't spoken to my dad in over a year, seen him in four. I have no idea where my brother is. I couldn't add anything of worth to her comment.

"I am sure Paul will keep your job open. He seems a shrewd guy. He wouldn't want to lose a good colleague."

"I don't plan on coming back to London, Craig."

My smile wound down like a vacuum cleaner turning off. I swallowed the information and pulled a wasp-chewing face.

"Well, you erm...you...of course you...are you erm...are you sure? So why then, exactly...why then won't you? Come back I mean...to London."

She sighed at the thought of a well-trodden path.

"The last six weeks, my life has taken a dive. First, I lost my boyfriend, then my flat, and with it the security of accommodation."

Been there, done that, I thought.

"I thought this job would be a step in the right direction and I could start standing on my own again, but my parents saw it as me avoiding responsibility. They feel I am wasting the education they paid for, which was very expensive to be fair."

Done that too.

"I've lost my social group, which was all through René in London. I'm drifting alone at the moment."

Check, next!

"And after Saturday, I don't even feel safe here any more. If I have no real friends, no family, no enjoyable job and feel unsafe, what is the point in me being here?"

Checkmate. Unguarded, I let out a smile.

"What are you smiling at? I'm serious."

"I know. Please don't think I am being unsympathetic, it's just..."

"Go on."

"You have pretty much just described me at the moment. Or at least how I have been feeling the last couple of weeks. But you know, today I don't feel quite so bad about it."

"How so? What is there to be positive about?"

"Listening to you describe some things, I instantly look on the brighter side of your situation. And I guess, when I make the link to my life, I can start to see all the things I have going for me." She looked bewildered. "For example, I am in a bit of a reverse situation to you with regards the job."

"What do mean?"

"I have a 'respectable' job, whatever that means. I earn good money and have certainly progressed from when I first moved to London."

"What did you do?"

"I worked in an organic food shop stacking fruit and veg."

"Did you have a reason?" It was a valid question, but I was embarrassed I had not been prepared for it.

"Maybe I was lazy, maybe I was trying to make a statement. But I didn't feel pressure from others to do something more. I should give myself credit, I had a stubborn streak."

"Why is that something to give yourself credit for?"

"I guess because I was more willing to do what I wanted. Not at the expense of others, but I had a single-mindedness which, thinking about it, is something I could do with now."

"Why did you stop listening to the stubborn streak?"

"The other voices got louder. I started listening to them, or felt like I should start listening to them, not sure which. I never consciously gave in, just did it bit by bit."

"What happened?"

"A few of the people who worked there, were prima donnas."

"What does that mean?"

"They felt that they were better than the job. Half of them did the job because it was easy money and they were lazy and had other plans, usually involving a band. I worked with so many wannabe musicians."

"What's so bad about that? They had a dream, no?"

"Yes they had a dream, but you can have a dream with dignity. Some of these people acted as if this work was below them: as if there was something wrong with it, and they were somehow worthy because they chose to avoid doing this work." She looked a little annoyed.

"And you were different from them?"

"I had respect for a job that I chose to do. If I take a job, then I have a certain responsibility to do it, because if it really is that bad, I should just leave. On the other hand, the company exploited many highly intelligent people. I worked with lawyers and doctors and people who owned their own businesses. Most of them were foreigners who wanted to learn English, hired by the firm because they were only allowed to earn a certain amount of money in England. This was totally at odds with the altruistic company image: organic and fair trade products aimed at left wing, save the planet/whale/rainforest you name it,

Guardian readers. At the end of the day like nearly all businesses it was about one thing, the bottom line. But some of the people I worked with, used this hypocrisy as an excuse to be lazy. In reality, they lacked the very principles they pertained to have in the first place."

"That's their choice, no?"

"Fair enough, but then there were people who were trying to do a good job, and their life was made much harder because some were just plain lazy. Where is the respect they deserve? You look unconvinced."

"I am. If the company was after just money, and doing it under the guise of organic living and fair trade, then I think they deserve what they get for that hypocrisy."

"I just think that these people waive the right to complain about that hypocrisy. If someone moans their employer is exploiting them and doesn't pay them enough, but at the same time that person is lazy and works sloppily, they don't deserve to be paid better. It's not like the company was a sweat shop. If it was that bad, at least they have the right to leave and find a better paid job, and there are plenty out there in London. However, if the company treats the hard-worker like shit, I feel they have a valid case to complain. People should have a bit of pride in what they do. I respect the people who collect our rubbish and shit up over night, especially in this city. I wouldn't want to do it."

"So why did you give it up and start selling?"

"I started to doubt myself and felt that everyone else can't be wrong. It takes mental strength to swim against the tide, more than I have."

"Don't many salesmen exploit people? Treat people differently, spend more time with rich people, less time with poor."

I felt an urge to find an excuse.

"That's where I am completely hypocritical." I smiled to cover up my shame. She focused on stirring her orange juice with a straw.

"I sometimes wonder, if we are growing up too fast." she said.

"What do you mean?"

"There is such a big difference between us and our parents, isn't there? They always seem unhappy or upset with me, or can't understand why I do something."

"Isn't that just the natural worries of parenthood?"

"I suppose so."

"I am sure it was the same with their parents, they probably worried about them as well. I remember my mum telling me of secrets she used to keep from her parents, like boyfriends and late night meetings in the park. And things her parents used to moan to my mother about my mother's generation." I thought fondly of my mother.

"But was this always so? Have parents always been complaining about their children's generation? If this was so, then parents in the 17th century were complaining about their children's generation, how they were reckless and without respect. I can't imagine that. Most of the time, children just followed in their parents footsteps, either boys following daddy or girls following mummy."

"They didn't have the choice that we have today. If someone moved from Amboise to London back then, it couldn't just be for a few months for experience." I tried to sound like she was doing something worthwhile, but it sounded more like I was suggesting she was spoilt.

"I am sure there were some people who went against the grain. It is a part of human nature to question what came before, no?"

"I guess so, but as time has passed we have become more individualistic, less community minded. It's all about what you can achieve on your own today. Hundreds of years ago...I don't know if I am romanticising this, but I get the impression people were driven to explore things in science not for personal gain, but more for, well, the good of mankind. Or because mankind had got it wrong."

"Maybe mankind has got it wrong today. Maybe we are wrong to go out and earn money for ourselves and our holidays and our nights out and parties."

"In the past, life was more out of survival and necessity. No other generation has had the possibility of doing nothing like we have." I became very conscious of having spent three weeks doing nothing in a café.

"Yes, but that instinct for survival is being eroded because life is not so hard."

"Eroded!" I was shocked.

"People don't have to survive as much today. Survival is easier because there are organisations to help them, a social system to fund them and people to donate money if they live on the streets." She had a point.

"For some people. But there are many people who do just 'survive'. Look at Thomas and his family. He had to travel halfway across the world to get money for his family – that's his own social system. He is just the tip of the iceberg as well. We have loads of people coming here from life or death situations across the world. I hope I'll never have to experience that kind of life. I just wish that some people didn't have such a lack of community respect that they go out drinking at night and then come home and piss against the door of my block of flats at two in the morning."

"So you do think your generation has less respect than previous generations."

"We've never had to deal with so many people before. How many people are in London, seven, eight million? That's too many people to be living together. Have you ever seen the film Crocodile Dundee? This Australian farmer comes from the wilderness to New York and is amazed that seven million people want to live together. Where he comes from, everybody wants to live together and he can't imagine living somewhere people don't. In London, everybody occupies the same space, but don't want to share that space with strangers who have completely different views and opinions and culture to them. It's a miracle there is as little crime as there is."

"You really don't like London do you?" Sympathy crept back into her voice.

"It's not that I don't like London. I'm very much of my generation in that I have few family ties and I like that. I've embraced my friends more than my family. It sounds a shame, but I think that we are getting more and more like that. Particularly as people travel further and further away from home. You said yourself you see your family less than you want."

"You never see yours, but yours are easier to get to."

"Well, there are reasons for that."

"Were they bad to you?"

"No."

"Then why?"

"There are lots of reasons."

"Could you tell me one?"

"My father had an affair."

"I don't understand."

"I don't like the way they dealt with it."

"You don't like how they dealt with it!"

"My dad cheated on my mum and I couldn't forgive him for that, and my mum just wanted him back regardless, as if he had done nothing wrong, and I couldn't respect her for that." I felt bare in front of her. I realised the affair was a product of the situation with my brother, but I hated mitigating his actions. "Do you think I am a bad son?"

"No. I can see why you are angry. However, it is their life. They are the ones who have to live with their decisions, not you."

"But it affects me. I was involved. Of course I have to think about how it involves me." I slumped at her silence.

"We have already had a disagreement talking like this. I don't want to offend you."

"I promise I won't get angry."

"All right. It is not your place to punish your father. You can choose what happens in your relationship with your father, but you are punishing the two of them if you never see them. Are they together again?"

"Yes."

"But you never go to see them?"

"No."

"So your mother, never gets to see her son as a result of your father's actions. What if your father realises he did something wrong and is genuinely sorry?"

"I don't know. But I can't just forgive him for cheating on her. He did something unforgivable."

"It's not always one way."

"What do you mean?"

"If everything was perfect, why would he need to have an affair?"

"This, from that same woman that said all men would have an affair if they felt they could get away with it."

Her blush waved a white flag.

"A wise man, who I think is being less wise at the moment, pointed out to me that that is simply not the case. I would like to chat some more, but I have to get back to work."

"Oh sure, are you working tomorrow?"

"Yes. We are usually quietest around eleven if you wish to come in and chat, or would you like to meet after work?"

I had waited nearly three weeks for her to say that, and yet I didn't feel excited. I felt like I had just stood up after drinking a bottle of wine in 5 minutes. I wonder if this is how affairs are ended. Do they cease to be exciting when accepted as a norm? When one of you finally suggests going out for dinner and being in public, does this anaesthetise you to excitement? I have never had an affair, and I only know one friend who has. Her name was Alex, and she ended up marrying the guy she had an affair with. She might have something to say against this hypothesis.

"I am in town tomorrow anyway, so I will just come here then."

As Marie-Louise walked away, I mulled over our conversation. Some of it seemed the opposite of what I had been discussing with Paul the previous day. Something he said must have stirred in me deep down. It reminded me of the person I used to be. Why do most people go the way I have gone when they get older? They call it growing up, as though to not do this is immature. Is this acceptance of acceptable behaviour just self-justification?

I got up and took my empty cup to the counter. Paul thanked me and I could tell he wasn't sour at me for my previous tantrum. As I left the café, I thought about Marie-Louise's plans to leave. I tried to imagine the café without her and reflected on one of the nicest conversations I had had with her. The café seemed sad, muted, as if holding its breath.

Chapter 23

After that day's chat with Marie-Louise, I lost myself in my own thoughts. It was like willingly entering a maze and paying no attention to my choice of direction. I was not even seeking the exit, simply following every turn to its logical conclusion and then starting again when each choice was exhausted. I fought off tiredness and sleep did not overwhelm me until after 3am. I arose early the next morning, fresh and re-energised. I had gained a little perspective from the chat and was starting to hypothesise some action. It had taken me a few weeks of bumbling antipathy, but when I awoke that morning, my exit from the maze had become a succinct goal, and an attainable one at that.

I wonder about the value of unproductiveness, and how periods of productivity often follow unfruitful ones. Often the fruitless periods are dismissed as worthless, especially with the myths of great art. We follow blindly the idea that great artists are subject to flashes of brilliance: on a whim they can change the world, produce great art, and move people emotionally for time immemorial. Newton's revelation came from an apple falling on his head. Kerouac sat down at a typewriter and wrote 'On the Road' in a handful of sittings. Great songs and paintings were supposedly born in the blink of an eye, and things were never the same again. I think people fail to recognise the hard work that goes into this process. How many pages does a writer throw away until he has a final copy? How many songs are disposed of before a truly great song is written? The end product is simply the culmination of the hard work involved. Like an iceberg, we never see the far greater part lying beneath the surface: we only see the awe inspiring tip.

I remember reading about 'Good Vibrations' by the Beach Boys, often put up on a pedestal within the realm of creative music. It took Brian Wilson over six months to perfect this piece of music that so many aspire to. It packs everything into a mere 3m39s. This is supposed to be the work of a genius at the peak of his powers, and nobody pays attention to those six months. The end product lasts for just over – one, seventy-one thousand eight-hundred and third of the time it took to produce! Mind you, I personally can't stand the Beach Boys. And the flip side of that song is the shit lyrics written by Mike Love. Despite having all that time to come up with them, he wrote them in the taxi ride over to the studio, and it shows.

As I stepped inside the café at ten clutching my new goal, Marie-Louise and Bobby K were talking. Only the Yahtzee group resided at a corner table.

"Here's the hero of the day. Man of the hour. Mr Muscle."

"Yes, thank you Bobby, autographs later."

"Sounds serious, man. Lou just told me she was shitting herself." His badly contracted sentences didn't shock me like his use of a swear word in front of her. And how come everyone had a pet name for her except me? Why was I not offered a short name?

"One minute Bobby, I did not say shitting myself, I said peeing myself." Although she was only repeating Bobby's choice of word, swearing doesn't sound right attached to a French accent. It detracts from the tonal beauty.

"Whatever it was, sounds like you came to keep company at the right time. What was with you? You have the runs as well?"

"It wasn't the most pleasant experience I have ever had."

"You were shitting yourself as well."

"Ignore him, Craig."

His baiting was interrupted by a sudden cry of Yahtzee.

"I simply hope it never happens to you Bobby. It's not something I would wish on my enemies, of which I might add, I do not class you as one." Why had I started talking like a university professor? In the presence of someone threatening my position, I do this a lot. Especially when faced with people who have money, physical power, or are fashion conscious, although I was not sure to which group Bobby belonged. There was something about using intellectually superior language that reinforced a feeling of intellectual superiority in me.

"Anyway, gotta shoot. Lou, Craig, must love and leave."

"Urgent appointment?" I tried to make an effort, but something about him just got my goat and there was more than a little sarcasm in my voice.

"Gotta see a man about a boat."

"In the middle of London?"

"In case you failed to notice, there's a very famous lock not one mile from this spot."

"What's that gotta do with you?"

"Ask me in 24."

The door worked its way back to its frame, and left me and 'Lou' centre stage. We smiled at each other as though remembering a shared precious moment. The door opened and pulled the spotlight to Donna.

"PPPLLLLLlllllllwweeeeee." At least, that was what it sounded like she said. It was definitely new vocabulary to me.

"Hey, Donna" I shouted.

She repeated her sound. Behind her, Matt was mouthing something to me. I was never any good at lip reading, but Marie-Louise got it straight away.

"Happy Birthday, Donna."

"Yes, happy birthday girl. How young are you today?" I quickly followed up.

"Weeee." It was high pitched and pricked our ear drums, but at least the windows stayed intact.

"How old is that, Matt?"

"Thirty-four."

I never imagined disabled people getting old. You never see 80 year-old disabled men in wheelchairs do you? I guess they were hidden away in the past and so we were not exposed to them. Exposed? I was talking about them like a disease!

"Would you like a birthday kiss, Donna?"

"Ooh. Donna, d'you hear that. Want a birthday kiss?" Matt chimed in.

I was unsure if she had understood the question, but she started rocking vigorously back and forth. I took that as a yes, and crouched down in front of her. She cocked her head to the side and spied me with her right eye. She gave me the turtle look again and extended her neck and consequently her cheek towards me. I pounced with a quick peck on her right cheek and followed it with a hug. It was a one-two boxing jab of affection and accompanied by some 'oohs' and 'aahs' from the others. Donna started to rock more violently. Strangely, I felt as if I was observing the scene as a fly on the wall and I was both surprised and proud of myself. My three weeks of feeble steps showed me she was a person who could experience enjoyment. She had things she liked and didn't like. She was just a little different in that she needed help doing them. But hey, there are times when I need help doing things. How would I feel if someone looked down on me just because I couldn't cook food, put a CD on, or go out for a walk on my own? And it also meant that I would appreciate someone giving me a hug or a kiss on my birthday.

"Drinks are on me."

"You don't have to do that, Donna has her own bunse." My mind flashed back to Saturday. I remembered lying face down on the floor, fearing for my own safety, unsure of what would happen next. The insecurity made me shiver. Money seemed the least important thing in the world.

"I know she does, but I want to buy a friend a drink on her birthday, you two as well."

"Cheers geezer. In that case, Donna'll have a cappuccino and I'll have a cuppa cha."

Marie-Louise got to making the drinks with a smile plastered on her face. I wanted to know the reason, but isn't that just the greatest invasion of privacy: to ask someone why they are smiling? It's like you can't have an unexpressed thought anymore.

"Make sure you get one for you. Have whatever you want." I was getting a kick out of this new wave of philanthropy. "And I want to get a cake for Donna." I turned to Matt who was tucking Donna up to a table. "Does Donna eat cake?"

"She eats anything." I had no idea where she put it: she was thin as a rake and I guess didn't do too much exercise.

"Do you mind if I spend a little time with the birthday girl?" It felt a little strange asking permission from Marie-Louise for this, but we had arranged to continue our conversation today.

"No, no problem. I can't take a proper break until when Paul comes in."

"Thanks." I took Donna's drink and cake over to her table and she greeted me with a raspberry.

"Well in that case, I will just take this cake back where it came from." I withdrew it slowly and I could see she noticed the disappearing treat. She slowly reached out her hand with a paper towel in it and started waving it frantically. "Oh I see! You're nice when you want it."

I slid the cake to her. She looked out the side of her head, elongating her neck. I imagined her saying, 'I need to remember this man. He gave me cake.' She gave a high pitched squeal and swapped her towel for a spoon. It was a cream cake with toasted almonds on top. She clearly favoured the cream part.

"Say, where d'you work Craig? Paul said you're off work at the mo'."

"Just round the corner. I'm a salesman for my sins. How long have you been at Donna's?"

"Nearly three years. About ten years all told in the NHS. I've worked in loadsa different homes."

"You must enjoy it, ten years."

"Yeah, guess I do. Missy here's sweet, but then all of 'em are."

"Is it a house, or a flat, or a hospital, or..." I tailed off as it struck me I was just naming buildings.

"They have their own house. It's the better alternative to the past where they were all locked away in institutions. They still need round the clock care, but as there are less people in these homes, they have more contact with carers and hopefully the community. They used to be in big mansions in the countryside, barely enough workers, no-one saw 'em, they saw no-one, and it was figured best for all."

"What's..." I started to form a question, but got very self-conscious.

"If you're worried being non-PC, don't. They change the correct terminology on a weekly basis. I never know what bloody phrase refers to what people nowadays."

"What's wrong with her?"

"She's learning disabled. There's hundreds of conflicting definitions, but basically she can't process information like we can. Donna has a physical disability called hemiplegia. She had a stroke when she was a kid and she's paralysed down her left side."

"Hence, the wheelchair?"

"Hence the wheelchair."

"But she...she seems a little slow. I mean, like she would struggle...I don't know. She can't talk for a start!"

"Well, yeah. The stroke buggered up her ability to learn."

"That's awful! How old was she?"

"I'm not sure exactly. I think about five or six. She was really young though."

"Can't she live at home?" At this point I saw a caramel coloured length of spit start a long descent from her lips towards the floor. It made about half the journey hanging onto her mouth before breaking away to jump the rest.

"She could. However, you can't just pop off to the cinema and leave her be, she needs 24-7 support. Parents can't usually give that. Either they have lack of money, time or just psychological ability."

"What do you mean by that?"

"Sometimes Donna can be a right pain in the arse, 'scuse my French. As can her friends, and all of us I guess. But most people don't realise Donna doesn't react from ignorance, but instinct. If she wants to take an hour to eat a piece of cake, some people might get pissed off at that."

"Surely her parents should have the psychological ability to deal with it. It's their child for Christ's sake." Matt smiled and took a second. Donna was slowly reaching to her coffee and we both watched, breathless as she brought it to her mouth and took a big slurp. I turned and caught Marie-Louise smiling at us. I perused the café – nobody else paid Donna any mind.

"Have you ever spent 24 hours with someone for a whole week."

"Er, no."

"Try it. A regular geezer would struggle with any other regular geezer. But if it were someone who needed constant care and wasn't so able to show gratitude or say thanks, I think you'd understand what I mean about psychological ability."

"Yeah, but you do it, and it's not even your kid." He leaned forward smiling. I felt like I was having a weakness analysed and exploited.

"But I get to go home. I don't work seven days a week. I have holiday. I get paid. And it's easier 'cos it ain't my flesh and blood. And I can walk away if I want to. AND it still gets tough at times."

"I guess so."

"You lookin' for a career change then?"

At this point several things happened. There was the sound of a smashing cup, my leg suddenly became wet, and I instinctively slid my chair back. Donna jumped forward and started shaking: she banged her arm against the table. She had dropped the cup, and the liquid on my leg was her coffee. Matt shot up, went round behind her and pulled her wheelchair back from the table. Two of the Yahtzee girls stood up from their chairs and were staring at the scene as if it was a street performance.

As Matt pulled Donna back, I noticed she was strapped in. It was obvious, but I had failed to notice it before. She was shaking violently, her eyes fluttering like flags in the wind and then her head lulled forward. I stood up.

"What's happening, does she need an ambulance, shall I call an ambulance?"

"No, it's dandy."

Matt started stroking the side of her head and talking to her softly, as if reassuring a wild horse. He continued this for a while.

"What's happening? It doesn't look fine."

Everyone was standing around, almost waiting for instructions. I could not believe that Matt didn't seem at all concerned. He continued stroking her.

"It's just a seizure that's all."

"JUST a seizure. Don't we need to get her to hospital?"

"She has 'em all the time, ease up mate." I started to see Donna's shaking was becoming less pronounced.

"That's all you need to do, stroke her?" I asked this question to the room.

He seemed to be shushing her. The shaking continued to decrease until it all but stopped. It seemed to last ages, but a glance at the clock showed it was about a minute. Matt turned to Marie-Louise.

"Could I take her in the office?"

She looked speechless. "Uh, sure. Go ahead."

Marie-Louise skipped ahead, opened the door and asked them if they needed anything else. Matt wheeled Donna through.

"No thanks, I just wanna get her cleaned up, then I'll take her home."

"Is she going to be all right?" I shouted this through the closing office door. Matt jammed his foot in the door.

"She's fine thanks mate, just tired that's all. I'll have to get her back in a bit."

The door shut and I saw people go back to their tables, discussing what they had seen. I felt useless.

"You got a mop to clean this up with?"

Marie-Louise nodded. "I'll help you."

I couldn't think of anything to say while doing it. I just kept thinking about Donna, helpless in that cage of a body. As if she didn't have a hard enough life as it was, she has to put up with seizures as well. Some birthday!

Chapter 24

Shortly after Donna and Matt left, Paul came in and said he had some things to discuss with Marie-Louise. I too had some things to discuss: with my manager. I decided while I was so near, I would go and see him to clear the air. I was not sure what to say, but I couldn't spend the rest of the week musing. I came back to the café a couple of hours later.

"How was it?" Marie-Louise asked.

"OK, I guess."

"And...did you resolve anything?"

"I told him how difficult the last few weeks had been. How I had not been acting consistently."

"And?"

"I told him that at the moment I had very little desire to come to work and sell. I also told him I was not sure if this was just a temporary feeling."

"What did he say?"

"He seemed keen to latch on to the temporary feeling part and said of course I had had a tough time, but I would get over it soon. He also threw me the 'plenty more fish in the sea' line. I told him I couldn't be sure whether I even wanted to continue selling, but I have a job for which I get paid, and a duty to earn my money; so I will go in Monday and continue to do my job, but if my feelings don't change, I will do something about it."

"What did he say to *that?*"

"I think he thought I was talking rubbish. I don't think he took me seriously, maybe he thought I was apologising or trying to get sympathy. He said I'd be coming up with more one-liners in no-time, and won't even remember Kate. He even talked about sending me on management training again."

"One-liners?" she said.

"Oh, just some stupid lines we come up with when selling to customers. It's surprising some of the shit we spout out without realising."

"Is management training something you want?"

"Absolutely not. I think it was just that he actually values me, or rather values my sales. When faced with losing an important part of his team he ignores everything I say and offers me something he sees as a reward. It's just part of the three management requisites."

"What are they?"

"The three things all managers have in common: they love the sound of their own voice; they are not interested in anything you say; and they think they are funny. He certainly does. We were in there for over half an hour and I spoke for about 5 minutes all told. The rest of the time was him trying to make me laugh, telling me about the tricks they had played on the new girl and how much I would soon realise what I had been missing. He didn't take on board anything I said."

"What kind of tricks?"

"Him and his assistant get the new girls, provided they are what they deem sexy, to go up ladders and clean the top-shelf TVs so they can 'hold the ladder' and look up their skirts."

"That's awful! Isn't that illegal?"

There was a time when I just wrote them off as sad whilst laughing; a time I found it funny. This was when I began at the firm and I was not willing to stand up and say it was wrong. I had a need to be liked by the manager, to be one of the gang. You turn away once, then you keep turning away and of course their behaviour is never denounced, so it keeps on happening. "When I started there I used to do it as well. Didn't have the balls to walk away. I just needed to fit in. Very sad I know."

She paused. Anything comforting she might think to say, we both knew I didn't deserve.

"I can't say that Paul fits your three management categories. He seems a genuinely nice person."

I looked over at him, sitting down with the old lady I had met a few weeks previously. When I had chatted to her, I felt completely out of place in The Kennedys. I was a salesman who was losing his girlfriend. Now I was single and didn't know how to define myself. I looked at Paul and thought about all the people who came into this café, who liked him and chatted to him like a friend. He was a bit like the conductor of an orchestra. We were the instruments, each one of us different, each contributing something unique to the café and all feeding off him.

With my job, there is some illusion that there is a friendship between seller and customer, but in reality it's money dependent. The more money they spend, the happier I am. I hate the conditional aspect of the relationship.

"You're right. He is a good manger, and more importantly a good man."

He looked over at me and caught my eye.

"Hey Craig, come over here."

As I walked slowly to the table, I wondered if the woman would recognise me.

"This is Mrs. Finch, I think you met each other a couple of weeks ago. She remembers you."

I extended my hand.

"Hi Mrs. Finch, how are you?"

"Irene please. You know, it doesn't matter how many times I ask him, he never calls me Irene."

"Got to respect your elders Mrs. Finch." Paul said.

"He's the only one I let call me Mrs. Finch. Well, them and the prison guards when I was inside."

My jaw dropped.

"You were inside. What on earth for?"

"My husband." She said this so matter of factly. I remembered from our conversation she mentioned her husband was dead.

"You...you..killed your...?"

They both fell about laughing.

"No, he was a prison warden. Worked in Holloway. Many years ago, I would visit him and take him lunch." I felt sick having just called an old lady a murderer. The laughter died down and she looked pleased at having fooled me.

"You were here when Donna had her seizure this morning. Tell Mrs. Finch about it will you."

"Mrs. Finch? Um, sure." I was bemused.

"Mrs. Finch is Donna's grandmother. She was supposed to meet her here for her birthday, but obviously Donna had to go home."

"Uh, she had a seizure. I have no idea what caused it. Matt seemed calm as anything. I thought it looked horrible. She looked so...helpless."

"Sadly Craig, she is epileptic. It's just part of her normal life. She usually has them a couple of times a week", Mrs. Finch said.

"A WEEK?"

"Yes, a week. Did she hurt herself or anything like that?"

"No, she didn't. Matt just said he would have to take her home to rest. Can you go and visit her?"

"I can, but I am not so keen to visit her in her home."

"Oh! Is there a reason?"

"One of the girls can be a little aggressive. I don't mind telling you I am a little afraid of her."

"What do you mean by aggressive?"

I could sense discomfort from Paul and he stepped in.

"One of the girls, Jenny, is a little unpredictable in her behaviour, and when she gets frustrated, she sometimes vents that on her environment, be it people or things. In the past, she has hit every one of the residents, most of the carers and even Mrs. Finch."

"Why on earth do they let her work there?"

They both started laughing out loud in a repeat performance. I had no idea what was so funny.

"Jenny is a client, not a carer." Paul said. I turned crimson.

"I shouldn't have got out of bed this morning."

"Don't worry Craig, you're not the first person to make that mistake."

"When she hit you, did she hurt you?" I was amazed people would want to work with someone like that.

"I was quite sore for a few days, I am not as fit as I used to be. I also think that outside visitors can disrupt her a little from her routine and she gets a little agitated. I just decided it would be better for everyone if I met Donna in the café instead."

"But surely Jenny can't just go around hitting people? Does she hit Donna?"

Paul took the baton again.

"These people have very little personal space or time. For their own safety, they need 24-hour support, but equally this gives them no time to themselves and they need stability and reassurance of protection. When Jenny hits out, she is usually either lacking stability, or feeling threatened. She doesn't just think, 'oh it will be fun to lay one on this woman here'. These people have very few constructed malicious thoughts. A lot of their behaviour is simply instinctual and they don't know or understand subtle, diplomatic ways of getting what they want."

Despite the intellectual questions queuing up in my mind, all I could manage was to purse my lips and offer a primitive outburst of air.

"Craig, what do you do when you feel unhappy about something?"

"Address whatever the problem is."

"Say a colleague annoys you at work. I don't know, steals a sale or something."

"Depends if it was deliberate or not."

"We'll say you think it was deliberate."

"If it was deliberate, I would do the same back. I guess try and lose them a sale or steal one of theirs."

"Very mature."

I felt very small.

"If I wasn't sure, I might talk to them about it. Find out if it was deliberate, subtly though."

"And now, what if you can't talk?"

"I wouldn't be much of a salesman would I?" Paul was looking at me with a deadpan expression. "All right. I guess I might somehow communicate with her using my bodily expressions and hope she understands."

"And if she doesn't understand. She does it again?"

"I guess I'd give her a slap."

"See. It's just you trying to say 'you stole my sale', and already you resorted to violence. It's the same for Jenny. She has limited means of communication, and the others have limited means of understanding or sympathy. Given that situation, of course sometimes they might express themselves with violent actions."

I sat back defeated. I realised the work that Matt and Paul did was not as much fun and games as it looked when they were in the café.

"So you could get beaten up any day? Every day you deal with that."

"Beaten up is a harsh word, but in theory, yes. In reality, it's really not like that, and 99% of their interaction is not violent."

"What do you do when it is?"

"Depends how you feel. If you're angry, walk away and remind yourself it's not personal. And of course try and solve the root of their frustration."

"Respect to you."

"It's not something I was born with, or had when I started work there. It takes time to learn that. You could learn it too, anybody could."

"I'm not sure. It's hard not to blame someone when they come for you with no reason."

"There is always a reason. When you take that on board the rest comes naturally."

We all paused reflectively.

"Anyway, I think we need a break. You want a coffee, Craig?"

"Please."

"And I think I had better head off home. I'll meet up with Donna tomorrow. It was nice to meet you again Craig, look after yourself. And don't worry, seizures are just part of her normal life."

"Thanks, Mrs. Finch, I'll remember that."

"Irene, please." I smiled, acknowledging my mistake.

Chapter 25

Paul relieved Marie-Louise. She came over with a coffee for me and a glass of milk for her. She sat down and started lotioning her hands. She was wearing a shirt with a larger neck hole, exposing more of her neck and revealing more red patches than I had seen before.

"You OK?" I said.

"A little tired from work. Still, I am a bit better."

"Have you had any more thoughts?"

"What about?"

"I guess about what you are going to do."

She looked down at her hands and then away to the counter.

"Well, I am definitely going to go back to Amboise for a while."

My heart began to compete with her for my attention. Her mention of leaving conjured up an image of an empty apartment. I had started to hold on to the café more than anything else. It had become my replacement girlfriend. The thing in which I invested my time, heart and energy.

"You can have my job if you want it." She was laughing, but I could tell there was a hint of seriousness about her.

"Come on. Could you see me in a place like this?" Despite the fact that my question was rhetorical, she was thinking carefully about an answer.

"Actually, yes."

"Really! Why?"

"For one, you are good with people. You can talk to anyone and everyone. I see that in the last few weeks, in how you have made good friends here. People like to be around you and spend time with you. We don't realise how much of a compliment it is when people want to spend their time with us."

"Friends. Like who?" God knows why I was getting defensive. She was paying me a compliment and I seemed unwilling to accept.

"Like Paul. Like Mrs. Finch. Matt and Donna. Bobby K."

"Bobby K can't stand me. I am not sure he likes anyone but himself."

"Actually, he thinks you are a decent guy. He told me today. He was asking about you and thought we were seeing each other."

"Really!" I tried not to sound too excited. "But working in a café, it's not exactly a career move is it? No offence."

"Oh, so all that yesterday about those colleagues feeling above their job status, that only counted for other people did it?" I could tell hers was a rhetorical question too, yet I felt compelled to answer.

"No, just..." I couldn't defend my statement. "OK. I admit it. At heart, I am just worried what people will think of it. And although I like to think that it doesn't matter, it would feel like a step back, like I should be doing better. I don't mean better. I can't find a word for what I really mean." I swallowed hard and could feel I was starting to well up. A tear trickled down my cheek. "I just have no idea what I should be doing. Or in fact, what I want to be doing. If I don't know what I want to be doing, how the hell can I make decisions? I mean really, what does it fucking matter what I do? No-one around me worries about it. My parents just want me to get in touch, my friends just want to see me. I am really lucky that none of them judge me like other people's friends would. And yet I feel like I would be a failure if I was my age and working in a coffee shop. What does that say about me really?"

"Craig, come here." She took my hands and pulled me closer to her. She threw her arms open and drew me in. I rested my head on her shoulder. The red patch of her skin felt rough and my tears ran directly onto it. At that moment, my chest seemed to pop and tears came flowing out. I could only repeat the word 'sorry', like a record with a scratch. She rubbed her hand up and down my back and her other hand over the back of my head. We stayed like that for a few minutes. Before that, I hadn't cried in about three years, since I left Bristol. When you don't cry, you drown inside.

I pulled back from her. I felt so much lighter, like shedding soaking clothes in your hallway after being out in a downpour.

"One thing is for sure. I plan to make that camping trip to visit you in Amboise. It sounds wonderful."

"You only have my word for it being beautiful."

"Actually I looked it up a bit on the net. It sounds lovely around there. I think also a holiday away from London might do me good. I haven't left this city in two years."

"That's too long to be stuck in a big city."

"So, when is the best time of year to visit?"

"I would say if the weather is not important then autumn is best. The weather is unpredictable, but the change of colours in the scenery is wonderful."

"When are you thinking about leaving?"

She looked away again. She pulled her knees together and placed her hands on them, sitting upright as if it were a job interview.

"I'm going back next week."

"Next week! You don't waste any time. So when do you finish here?"

"Actually, it's my last day today."

A pounding started in my head; a next door neighbour doing renovation. My mouth was dry and needed watering. I reached out for her milk and gestured to ask if it was OK to drink some. She nodded and I took a mouthful.

"Next week! Does Paul know? Have you told Paul?"

"Yes. I have been talking with him about it everyday this week. I am not absolutely convinced, but I don't want to walk around fearing for my safety and I think I need some time away from these memories and distractions to deal with me and René, you know?" I just shrugged my shoulders and offered my open palms up to the ceiling.

"I know it's sudden, but I feel like there is a great weight on me at the moment. Everywhere I go it's pushing me down and I can't escape it. It is London. Not just London, but everything that is related to it. All the memories are tied in with it and I can't think of anything good about it."

"What about The Kennedys? Is that not good?"

"Working here has been one of the bright spots. I just wish that it had come at a different time, like when I first arrived in England. Or if Saturday hadn't happened I might be strong enough to deal with it, but it's just taken everything I had left. I need to recharge."

I paused. I was wondering whether I should say something to her. It was clear to me, now that I was on the brink of losing her, that I really did want her. I ached to be with her.

"Plus, I have started to have feelings for someone." When she said this it was like the final breath of air being blown into a balloon before being let go of. My mouth was making fish-like gulping movements. I realised for the last couple of minutes I had been avoiding eye contact. I got her back in my focus, though it hurt to do so.

"Can I call you Lou now, or do you prefer something else?"

"Actually I don't really like nicknames. I always liked the fact that you called me by my proper name."

"Marie-Louise it is then. Listen, I have a confession to make. I realise I have spent a lot of time in this café in the last few weeks, and I really love the place, but there was another reason for me coming back so often."

Then she started smiling. My heart skipped a beat and I was lying in a sunbeam aimed exclusively at me.

"Craig, you have been a really great person to talk to since I came here. You have been the biggest bright spot in this place. But I can't stay only because I have feelings for you. I don't think it is enough at the moment. There are too many negatives for me in London."

"But if I feel this way as well then you have to stay. I mean not necessarily here at work, but in London."

"I have no idea how things would turn out. It would be a big gamble that I don't really want to bet my mental health on."

"Ever since I met you, I wanted to talk to you more and alone, but there was always something in the way." I cursed all those missed opportunities.

"But I knew you had just split up with your girlfriend, and I was in a similar situation. I thought it seemed a little foolish."

"Foolish is good. People should do more foolish things. I can do foolish."

She chuckled. It was an untroubled laugh and I realised that I had done that: I had touched her. She said I had touched a lot of people in this café, but if that was true, they had touched me too. The café both gave and received in that manner. Jam Man, the Yahtzee girls, Bobby K, Thomas, Matt, Donna, Mrs. Finch: the one thing all these different people had in common was this café. These people from all over the world, from different generations and walks of life, all came to The Kennedys to share the place and share a bit of each other. The café too was reliant on them. Each of them was an integral part of its charm. I thought about meeting Kim the next day. It was becoming a regular place for us to meet, at least in the context of the regularity in which we meet. Yet tomorrow would be a day without Marie-Louise. She was not the sole reason I had come to the café, I would be back, but she would be sorely missed. The Kennedys was like a tree and I was the ground, and each day I spent here, each coffee I drank, each new person I met, was another root winding itself into me, embracing and clinging on to me. I fed it, and it fed me.

"One thing is for sure, I will definitely have to come and visit you now. You said you could find a good campsite, didn't you? Although I am not sure I can wait until the autumn."

"You will be welcome any time." She laughed again.

"Now all I have to do is buy a tent."

Chapter 26

The next day, I entered the café and considered all the times I could have experienced an epiphany in the previous few weeks: breaking up with Kate; going to the doctor's; being held hostage in a robbery; Marie-Louise's statement of intent to leave; even our rather muted goodbye. The list was plentiful. Yet all these events had passed me by with seemingly little effect, and as I walked into The Kennedys on Friday, that was when I experienced it: the realisation of having grown up. It didn't equate to full acceptance, but it was the first step.

When Marie-Louise had left the previous day there was a small queue of people wanting to say goodbye. In the midst of all of these, we settled for a hug and a knowing look. It expressed our knowledge that we would meet each other again soon. It was not enough when placed alongside what I wanted, but it was a start, and drew a line in the sand between Kate and me. I had finally had a day where I didn't feel sorry for myself. Not only that, it was a day I felt positive about what the future may hold. I had renewed energy, and felt ready to start back at work.

I held this feeling close as I strolled in to The Kennedys just before twelve. The Yahtzee group looked up at me and I gave them a clear hello; they smiled and reciprocated. There was nobody else I recognised, except Paul behind the counter.

"You're a little early for your shift. Trying to score some brownie points with the new boss."

"I told you, I am meeting Kim at twelve."

"So you did. You can start by getting your own drink though, I'm desperate for the toilet."

"I think I can stall people until you come back."

As Paul left me alone, I walked behind the counter and looked out at the people. I felt a sense of place: a justification to my being there. As I was admiring the clientèle, the door opened and in bound Marie-Louise's friend I had met on the day of her migraine.

"Ah, Cregg! 'Ow are you?"

"Fine thanks. Forgive me, but I can't for the life of me remember your name."

"Laura."

"I'm sorry Laura, but you have missed Marie-Louise by one day."

"Oh, I know that is right. But I want to come by as I work in the near. You are working here now, very nice! Can I have a coffee with a lot of milk please to go."

"Coming right up. Where do you work?"

"There is a restaurant on Parkway, near the park. I am a waitress there. Chambord, you know it?"

"Can't say I do. You on a lunch time shift?"

"I work the whole of the day, but I start today a little later as I see Marie-Louise this morning."

"We'll definitely miss her in here."

"I too. She is a good friend."

Paul came back to the counter, took one look at Laura and registered the previous meeting with her.

"Laura, lovely to see you back in here. And in better circumstances this time as well."

"Yes, it was a quick visit last time. Truth is, until Marie started working here, I had never known about this place. But now it is on my way to work I will come in."

"I will have to save you a seat then."

Kim walked in and looked enquiringly at me standing behind the counter. Paul continued his line of conversation about work with Laura and I walked back round to greet Kim. We hugged and I held on longer than usual.

"I was in need of that." I said.

"What's happening in your life at the moment? It seems to be changing with the wind!"

"Huh! Oh, the apron. In a minute. First I want to say thanks for your support. And despite all my attempts to get rid of my friends recently, I don't plan on keeping that practice up; I appreciate you coming. How was the exam?"

We took a seat.

"Actually, pretty awful."

"In what way?"

"They really provoked me for a reaction – one guy in particular – and never let up. I think I made it apparent; I lost my temper with them in frustration."

"How did you lose your temper?"

"One of the guys is a specialist in East African countries and seemed to be making wild comparisons to his specialities and then making wild statements of disbelief whenever I said something he didn't know. The one who is a specialist on Mali, seemed to leave it up to the others, and the third actually said on two occasions – 'I think you may be getting ahead of yourself on that matter', in the most autocratic way imaginable. 'Getting ahead of yourself' – can you believe that?"

"I can't begin to believe how you must be feeling. The level of knowledge you must have to even get into a situation like that seems somewhat out of my reach. Surely it wasn't that bad, though?"

"You don't know these guys. With some of them, it is not so much about challenging your credentials, as much as building a brick wall around theirs."

"Sure it wasn't just a ruse to try and get a rise out of you?"

"If it was it worked. Why did I have to pull that prick Sanders? That could cost me my scholarship. If that goes, I am really up shit's creek. No way Dad is going to chip in to save this ship if it takes a hit."

"If it comes down to money, don't worry. I can always help you out."

"You can't afford to help me out any more than Marlise." he said.

"First of all, wait and see what happens. You could be just over-dramatising it. Second, I'll decide if I can afford it. I have something that I have been saving for an emergency. Seems like this could be one of those situations. You have put so much of yourself into this, I for one am not going to let you throw it away. I admire the level of dedication and enthusiasm you have to your subject. If I had something like that, I would not let it go to waste. Sadly, I have no exceptional knowledge of anything, but still."

"Not exceptional knowledge, but there is something to be said for being an exceptional person."

"I wouldn't say I am there either. It's a nice goal, though." I said.

"Even if you aren't there that doesn't stop you trying. One thing I always admired in you, is that you were never happy standing still. I don't mean in the materialistic way, but as a person. You were always trying to better yourself."

"I lost that for a while, didn't I."

"You got it back you think?" he asked.

"I realise, I got complacent with Kate. It was not fair to anyone to stop trying to improve myself. I know I did her a disservice, but truthfully, I am more pissed off with doing myself a disservice, although I guess they are rather intertwined. I've been a real arsehole, for a long while." For a second I stared at a coffee stain on the table. It had an inner and outer ring, almost like a layer of skin. I licked my finger and rubbed it, but it was very stubborn and only the outer ring rubbed off. "I just want to be a better person."

"See what I mean. That takes real courage to say that."

"Shouldn't everyone want that?"

"It's for exactly the reason that most people don't want to do that, that makes that an exceptional goal. Most people think they are there already. True, if you ask them if they think they are perfect, they would say of course not, but not many people would come out unprompted and say 'I want to be a better person.'"

We sat there in silence for a while, warming to each other's company again.

"Marie-Louise has left. It was her final day yesterday."

"You miss her, huh?"

"Oddly, I think it is quite healthy that she has left. She is going back to Amboise. I said I would go with her to the airport and we could have a coffee together – somewhere new. And we agreed that I will go and visit her next month." I was suddenly aware at how much I had been spewing my feelings all out in Kim's direction. The momentary guilt was eclipsed when I looked right at him and noticed how much attention he was paying to my words. "We'll see what happens, but I feel...excited. I had forgotten what that was like."

"Still, it's a bummer she has left, especially if you two hadn't had a chance to start something."

"But on the other hand, I realise that I have a tendency to put all my eggs in one basket. The last couple of years with Marie-Louise just got too damn claustrophobic. Even now, I had started to do the same with this café. At least with Marie-Louise in another country, I have minimum two baskets to focus on."

"You realise you just said Marie-Louise instead of Kate."

"Really!" I felt the blood rush to my cheeks to accompany my embarrassment. "I guess she has got a hold on me."

"And what about Kate? You spoken to her?"

"That's something that will have to take a natural course. I don't hate her, not by a long shot. But I am not in a position to be friends yet. Besides, it would seem so contrived. If we bumped into each other down the road I might feel different, but at the moment, it seems like a friendship with her is something that we would really have to work on, and I have plenty of other things to be working on at the moment."

"While we are on this eggs in the basket theme, do you think it is such a good idea working here then? Aren't you just building a foster home for yourself?"

"Working here!" I laughed at the misunderstanding and tried to imagine what my manager might say if he walked in and saw me wearing an apron.

"I am just helping Paul out since Marie-Louise left at such short notice. I go back to work on Monday, but until then, I have a little time to help out Paul. Anyways, I get a free coffee when I am on shift so can't complain. I don't start for another hour, but let me grab us a drink. Chai tea and an espresso, yeah?"

"With soya milk and honey please, no sugar."

"Does that actually taste of anything? It sounds so empty."

"You get used to it I suppose."

"Where is the fun in having to get used to a drink?" I asked.

"I know it's good for me. I guess a part of me likes liking something a little different."

"I imagine everyone takes the piss out of you for it."

"They do, but you get used to that as well. There's comfort in repeated discomfort."

I asked Paul if I could get us our drinks and took my time. I fished around the different levels of roast he had under the counter and picked up the 'Yin-Yang'.

"What's this roast, Paul?"

"It's a blend: half Midday, half French. You get the fruity flavour of the Midday with the punch of the French. Try it."

"I think I just might."

Being on the working side of the counter was a little like being on a stage at a primary school play, with all the parents waiting for their child's one line. Every so often, the parents look up hoping to be entertained, and very often this entertainment comes from the most unusual sources. Paul sometimes just bursts into song along with something on the stereo and the patrons smile whilst looking at each other for reassurance that they did not just imagine something. Or he might greet someone enthusiastically using one of the eleven different language greetings he has picked up over time. Or when someone is alone and looks up at him he starts doing a quasi-Bryan Brown impression from the film *Cocktail*, only adapted to the coffee counter. I too felt the pressure to perform, but as I looked out, the faces were thankfully buried in conversations and books.

I took the drinks back to the table, and heard a lone cry of Yahtzee. The girls were smiling at each other. Jam Man had not long arrived and was at the counter spreading some jam on a muffin to offer to Paul as they chatted away. People walked past the café outside, completely detached from it. They had probably never been here, might never come. I couldn't help but feel there was something a little sad about that. Everybody needs somewhere they can feel at home.

About the Author

Shaun was born and raised in south-east England. During his teenage years only his obsessions with R.E.M. and baseball stood out. He left town to pursue his non-practical dream of obtaining a liberal arts degree but got distracted on the way; he bought a guitar, taught himself to play and write songs and started performing around Birmingham. He left the University of Wolverhampton in 2001 with a degree in American Studies which affirmed an oft ignored feeling that he had been born on the wrong continent. He continued to write, perform and record music whilst holding various bill-paying jobs until 2005 when he fell in love with a German and moved to her home town of Mainz. They later married and now have a young daughter. Soon after arriving in Germany he exchanged writing songs for longer texts and eventually began his first novel *London, in Limbo*. Shaun is an English Teacher and is now working on the difficult task of three second novels.

Thanks to Verena for the cover design, all those people who read it and gave me feedback, and Alvimann from morgueFile for the front cover image.

If you found this book enjoyable please spread the word.

Connect with Shaun Girling:
Wordpress: http://www.londoninlimbo.wordpress.co[1]m
Smashwords: https://www.smashwords.com/profile/view/shaungirling

---

1. http://www.londoninlimbo.wordpress.com/

www.ingramcontent.com/pod-product-compliance
Lightning Source LLC
Chambersburg PA
CBHW031501160726
47994CB00005B/2132